The Secret Scrolls

The Secret Scrolls

SONIA FALASCHI-RAY

Matador
9 Priory Business Park,
Wistow Road, Kibworth Beauchamp,
Leicestershire. LE8 0RX
Tel: 0116 279 2299
Email: books@troubador.co.uk
Web: www.troubador.co.uk/matador
Twitter: @matadorbooks

ISBN 978 1785890 437

British Library Cataloguing in Publication Data.
A catalogue record for this book is available from the British Library.

Printed and bound in the UK by TJ International, Padstow, Cornwall
Typeset in 11pt Aldine401 BT by Troubador Publishing Ltd, Leicester, UK

Matador is an imprint of Troubador Publishing Ltd

I dedicate this book to The Reverend Nicky Gumbel, Vicar of Holy Trinity Brompton, and to his wife Pippa. In my view Nicky, ably supported by Pippa, is the foremost evangelist of our generation. His leadership and development of the *Alpha* course, which has enabled so many people throughout the world to be enfolded into the love of God through Christ Jesus in the power of the Holy Spirit, cannot be overestimated. I feel privileged to have been brought through it to a living faith at HTB in 1998.

CONTENTS

CHAPTER 1

Sicily

Wednesday

'Cabin crew, ten minutes to landing. Ladies and gentlemen, this is your captain speaking. The temperature in Syracuse is seventeen degrees Celsius, cloudy with a light westerly breeze.'

Verity Hunter glanced out of the window, which gave her an uninterrupted view of the wing. She smiled to herself and looked over at Dr Crispin Goodman, who was shutting down his iPad from aeroplane-safe mode. He was slim, good looking, with slightly sandy hair and a trim moustache. Aged twenty-seven, he had a post-doc research post at Corpus Christi College, Cambridge, having just completed his PhD on Roman catacombs. He had been recommended to assist her in some historical technicalities of her trip and they had first met at the airport, having exchanged a couple of emails.

Verity had read classics at Merton College, Oxford. During the graduate recruitment fair she was attracted to commerce and so trained as a management accountant, initially working in the finance department of English Heritage. From there she had been head-hunted to become the Director of Finance for the Poghosian Foundation, a charitable trust created by a philanthropist whose family found sanctuary in London, having fled Armenia during the Ottoman persecution of 1915.

Grigor Poghosian's passion was to preserve and restore cultural, and particularly religious, buildings. Verity had come to Sicily to investigate the progress of a restoration project for

1

the catacombs of St John the Evangelist in Syracuse, managed by Kairós, the Papal Commission for Sacred Archaeology, which administered the ruined church and catacombs, and to which the Poghosian Foundation had given a substantial grant. Judging by the evasive progress reports and fuzzy photos, not much had been achieved, either in restoring the collapsed tunnels and damaged sarcophagi, or in the refurbishment of the visitors' centre. However, all the funds had been drawn down and a request for further assistance received.

The landing and passage through passport control were uneventful. Scanning the arrivals lounge, Crispin saw a swarthy, squat young man holding up a sign with *Goodman* written on it.

'There he is!'

Verity winced. How typical of people to assume that Crispin was in charge, merely because he was male. She strode up to the man holding the sign and said firmly, in Italian, 'I am Verity Hunter and this is my *assistant*, Dr Crispin Goodman.'

'Marco Sodano. I work with *Il Direttore*, Dr Augusto Gargallo. He sends his regards. My car is outside.' He addressed this to Crispin, ignoring Verity. On shaking hands, he held Crispin's graze fractionally longer than necessary, absorbing his sky-blue polo shirt, sharp chinos, tan brogues and butter-soft tan leather bomber jacket. Crispin appeared far more elegant than most academics; he could almost be taken for an Italian. Marco led the way to a battered two-door Fiat Punto.

Verity turned to Crispin. 'Do you mind if I sit in the front? I tend to feel car-sick in the back.'

Crispin smiled, gallantly clambered behind the front seat, and folded himself up. Marco forcefully dumped their bags in the boot and got in, glancing distastefully at Verity. He knew why they were there and it could prove an uncomfortable visit for all concerned.

Catania airport was an ugly concrete monolith, but they soon pulled out onto a superb modern highway. Despite its being a working day, there were not many cars and fewer lorries. The road seemed over-designed for the traffic volume. EU money no doubt, thought Verity, but at least it had been built.

It was mid-September and the first rains had fallen after a long, dry summer, just giving the new grass a chance. The sky was grey and dreary. Looming ahead was a huge blue and yellow IKEA sign. Crispin felt a pang of homesickness. He shared a small Victorian two-up, two-down terraced house just off Mill Road, Cambridge, with his partner, Hilary. It was IKEA'd to within a centimetre of Stockholm. Hilary worked as a lawyer in London, cycling to the station daily to catch the fast train to King's Cross. They had been able to put down a deposit on the house due to a couple of small legacies left to Crispin by his grandfather and elder brother, Hector. The mortgage was paid by Hilary.

'You speak good Italian,' commented Marco to Verity.

'Yes, my mother came from Milan.' As soon as she said this Verity could have kicked herself – the Italian north-south divide made Yorkshire playing Surrey at cricket look cuddly in comparison. Her remark would not smooth relations. Conversation remained stilted, as neither party wished to broach the reason for their visit.

The road wound through gentle hills, divided up into uneconomically sized fields, as inheritance laws required a split in land ownership. Oleander and cactus lined the motorway sporadically. Arriving at the outskirts of Syracuse, they passed a huge necropolis on their left – hundreds upon hundreds of monuments, partially concealed behind a grey wall. Bypassing signs to the port and Ortigia, the attractive and touristy peninsular that had made the whole town a UNESCO Heritage Site, they drove left up the hill towards the older Greek city, with its archaeological remains and theatre. Marco parked at Hotel Hermes, which was a soulless, commercial establishment rather than a welcoming tourist haven, where Verity had booked their rooms.

'*Il Direttore* told me that we will meet you for drinks in the upstairs hotel bar at seven and then eat at the hotel. You can discuss everything. OK?'

This again was addressed to Crispin. Marco then departed, without glancing at Verity.

'Signora Oonterr, welcome. Your passport please.' Verity's mouth twitched as she heard the receptionist struggle with her name. She had a friend Hugh who, whenever he visited Italy, was always called 'Oogg'.

They had adjacent rooms on the fourth floor overlooking the archaeological site and a sports complex. The church of St John the Evangelist was only one block away. They agreed to meet at 6.30 to confirm their strategy for their first encounter with Dr Augusto Gargallo, the director of Kairós.

Verity and Crispin were in the bar sipping Campari sodas when Dr Gargallo arrived with a sullen Marco in tow, late, flustered and apologetic. Gargallo looked haggard and anxious. He was a sparely built man of average height and wore scuffed shoes, a non-descript suit and a plain blue tie.

'Signora Oonter.'

'Please call me Verity, *Direttore*.'

'*Piacere, Verity, vero*, truth, *no?* So Augusto, please. And you are Crispin, as in Santo Crispin mentioned in your Shakespeare *Henry V*, no? *Scusami*. My English is not so good,' he claimed with excessive modesty, 'but I have seen the play in Italian.'

'Yes, I was born on the day of the battle of Agincourt, twenty-fifth of October, hence Crispin. I'm sorry I don't speak Italian.'

Crispin's knowledge of Italian extended little beyond the pizza menu, but he found that by listening carefully he could follow a conversation by mentally translating it into Latin. Although he had specialised in ancient Semitic languages at Liverpool University, he had been required to study Latin and Greek in his first year.

Verity was anxious to get down to business, but could tell that Augusto was equally anxious not to. She bided her time. Tomorrow they could go on site, see what had been achieved, go through the accounts and try to come to some kind of reconciliation.

The restaurant's menu was a mixture of international cuisine with a few Sicilian specialities. Antipasti were laid out on the buffet bar for self-service. Augusto chose a bottle of local red, Aquilae Nero D'Avola, and a white, Mandrarossa Costadune, along with sparkling water. They selected their antipasti, with Augusto studiously avoiding eye contact.

'Marco tells me you speak excellent Italian.'

'He is very kind. My mother came to Oxford to improve her English, fell in love and married a classics student, Gerald Hunter.'

Augusto smiled, understandingly. The main courses arrived: Verity's swordfish in an olive, wine, tomato, herb and garlic sauce, Augusto's local fish, sgombro, came simply grilled with lemon and herbs. Marco had a rare steak and Crispin chose veal cooked with slivers of cured ham, garlic and olives. They ate mostly in silence, as each attempt at casual conversation withered.

Augusto's mobile rang. '*Pronto. Si … Si … Stasera? In venti minuti? Qui? Certo Signore. Niente problema. Abbiamo quasi finito. Arrivederci.*' He quickly relayed the message. 'Cesare Romano is dropping by to meet you here shortly in the bar downstairs. He owns the building company doing our restoration and the refurbishment of our visitors' centre.'

Verity sensed the heightened tension, with both Augusto and Marco becoming edgy. Augusto ran his fingers through his thinning grey hair and gestured for the bill, despite not having finished dessert. He's frightened of this man, she thought.

Descending in the lift to the lobby bar, Verity and Crispin could do little but exchange glances. As the four of them were settling themselves into low leather sofas, with the bartender approaching, the revolving door spun and in strode a man they assumed to be Cesare Romano, followed closely by a glamorous-looking woman.

'*Direttore, Direttore,* so sorry to disturb your dinner, but I couldn't wait a moment longer to greet our illustrious guests,' Cesare exclaimed. Turning to Verity he extravagantly lifted her proffered hand to his lips and kissed it. She was assailed by a combination of expensive cologne, gel from his slicked back Berlusconi-style hair and a whiff of perspiration. '*Molto piacere, bella Signora*, honoured to meet you, and so beautiful,' he effused.

Cesare had a bull neck, chunky shoulders, was of medium height, and had a waistline that had lived well. The straining buttons on his monogrammed cream shirt deserved to be mentioned in dispatches. A large, gold St Christopher medallion on a chunky chain nestled in his dark, abundant chest hair. He wore a shiny, steel-grey slub-silk suit, which had fitted him better two centimetres ago, hand-made crocodile-skin loafers and a solid gold Rolex Yachtmaster. On his fourth finger was a heavy gold wedding ring and on his little finger a ring with a diamond, perhaps not quite as big as the Ritz but certainly at Cipriani Hotel level. He had dark, shrewd eyes and, Verity suspected, a darker, shrewder mind.

He perfunctorily shook Crispin's hand and ushered the woman forward. 'My personal assistant, Maria Rizzi,' he announced. Verity and Maria eyed each other with instant, mutual dislike. Verity, in her navy tailored trouser suit, turquoise silk shirt, simple gold necklace and mid-heel sandals faced a brunette in full slap, with big hair and a magnificent bosom straining against a leopard-skin patterned top. She sported shiny metallic lycra leggings, vertiginous heels and enormous Versace jewellery with Medusa-hinged sunglasses perched on her head.

Cesare brushed aside the proffered drinks list with '*Cognac per tutti!*'

Marco caught Crispin's startled gaze and winked. He sat next to him on the squishy sofa so their thighs could just touch.

'I am delighted to meet you, *Signor* Romano,' said Verity, with more warmth than she felt. He was going to be a handful and she was beginning to suspect where some of the restoration money might have gone.

'Cesare, please call me Cesare – and may I call you Verity?'

'Of course.'

At that moment a bottle of Hine Antique XO premier cru cognac arrived and the ritual of pouring proceeded in silence as each planned their next move. Augusto appeared to have shrunk. I wonder what hold Cesare has over him? Verity thought.

'Tomorrow we'd like to go to the catacombs and see what progress has been made, both to the visitors' centre and to the restoration of some of the tunnels. We were fascinated to read that you had discovered some unknown frescos near the entrance, which had been whitewashed over, and very much look forward to seeing those too.'

Verity addressed this speech both to Cesare, who was expansively reclining with a glass of cognac in one hand, his other on Maria's knee, and to Augusto, who looked more crumpled than ever.

Cesare nodded. '*Certo* Verity, of course, plenty of time for that. First we must show you the sights of Syracuse. Never let it be said that Sicilians do not know how to entertain their honoured guests properly.'

'No really, we don't have much time and would like to get

on and go through the accounts with you.' Verity glanced over at Crispin for support, but he seemed distracted, seemingly by Marco.

'There will be plenty of time for that. Maria and I will show you the sights of Ortigia. It has a fascinating history you know, with Grecian temples within churches and *palazzi*. Augusto will prepare everything for you to look at later. Won't you, Augusto?' Cesare's geniality was tinged with menace. 'I'll send Volpe over to help you tomorrow.'

'Of course, Cesare.' Augusto did not appear to be thrilled at the offer of Volpe's help.

At that moment a waltz ringtone sounded. Verity recognised it as the one played in the Visconti film, *The Leopard,* when Burt Lancaster, as an ageing Sicilian prince, dances with Claudia Cardinale, playing the buxom daughter of a jumped-up nobody who would become a 'big noise' in the new, unified Italy. She was destined to marry the prince's nephew. The film had been based on Giuseppe di Lampedusa's semi-autobiography.

Cesare's demeanour changed abruptly. He struggled up from the deep sofa and strode outside. Verity thought Maria looked troubled and she tried to make conversation, to little effect. Marco edged up to Crispin, who took it in good part. Cesare returned smiling, but clearly it had not been a welcome call.

'Now we must go. We will pick you both up from here at nine-thirty tomorrow morning.' Cesare clicked his fingers at the barman and, indicating the drinks, extracted from his back trouser pocket a roll of large denomination euros, peeled off several and waved aside proffered change. He once again ostentatiously kissed Verity's hand, nodded to the men and swept out, with his right hand planted proprietarily on Maria's bottom. A black S-Class Mercedes slipped away. Augusto and Marco took their leave, Crispin having extracted himself from

Marco's offer of a drink in a discreet little bar down the road.

Outside their rooms they paused to take stock.

'This could prove even trickier than I realised,' said Verity.

'Yes, Augusto looked wretched. I know he appointed Cesare's firm to do the work following a tendering process, but I wonder how much choice he really had, given how overawed he is by him,' responded Crispin.

'I checked him out before we came, as I was worried about getting involved in a Mafia-controlled building firm, though here that may be impossible to avoid. Cesare didn't appear too compromised. His firm has been reliable in the past, though the recent recession has hit profitability. He doesn't seem short of the readies.'

'Perhaps he has a number of business interests, not just building,' speculated Crispin. 'What time shall we meet up tomorrow?'

'Let's meet in the restaurant for breakfast at eight and hope our sightseeing trip isn't too extensive. They seem keen to keep us away from the church. Augusto's office suggested a fancy tourist hotel in downtown Ortigia and seemed very put out when they found I'd booked this one.'

They turned to unlock their doors, and Verity's gaze slid down Crispin's well-defined buttocks as he disappeared. Get a grip! she thought. That is just so unprofessional, and I've no idea about his domestic arrangements. Verity had recently finished a five-year affair with Graham, who was, at forty-six, fifteen years her senior – a charming, delightful, international-banking, commitment-phobe. She had ended it, but did feel a touch of the Bridget Joneses.

Verity was just under medium height and mostly a size fourteen. Smaller, when she bought those flattering Jaeger suits in the sale and alas, larger, with more fashionable brands. She struggled with her weight, enjoying good food and wine and, apart from the comfort-eating, was always trying – and generally failing – to lose those extra six kilos. She had well-cut, short dark-brown hair, hazel eyes and her mother's olive complexion, which tanned easily but could look sallow after a British winter.

She checked her emails, sent her mother a quick text and looked again through the reports she had been sent, purporting to show the project's progress. Playing for time, clearly, but they couldn't have thought that the Poghosian Foundation wouldn't send someone to check, could they? She deliberately chose to sleep on the side of the huge double bed next to where the phone wasn't, calculating that all its previous occupants would have chosen the telephone side and that the mattress had probably never been turned. Setting her phone alarm for 7.00, she switched out the light.

★ ★ ★

Crispin flung his jacket on a chair and removed his shoes. He phoned Hilary. 'Hi, it's me. How are things?'

'OK here, just started a new project. Company codename Tinbox wants to take over codename Biscuit. Shows they think it's a done deal. It will be fascinating, as there are various conflicts of interest and some rather ambiguously worded contracts. Oh and Tarquin presented me with a dead rat this morning. There on the back doorstep. Looked delighted. Tarquin I mean. I couldn't decide which wheelie bin it was destined for, so finally I chose compost.' Tarquin was a bruiser of a ginger tom cat who had adopted them shortly after they'd moved in. 'How's your day been?'

'Verity got her nose put out of joint by my name being held up by the chap sent to meet us. I had a crippling journey from the airport, crunched in the back of the smallest car ever. Now we're facing obfuscation and cover-up, but we expected that. Met the sleaziest Sicilian with his floozy, sorry, "personal assistant", and he seems to be calling the shots. He insists on taking us sightseeing tomorrow, when certainly Verity would rather be getting to grips with the project. It's frustrating but I doubt it'll be dull. Do you have any other news?'

'Yes, your mother phoned, something about coming to visit. It was sticky as I had to pretend I was just a friend staying here and not "Hilary". Crispin this has got to stop! I won't live in the shadows like this, unable to answer my own phone. You've got to sort yourself out and tell them. They probably know deep down, so it would come as a relief.'

'I don't think so.'

'Anyhow, I'm sick of it, to the extent I really wonder if we can go on together like this. I'm off to a party tomorrow night, no doubt having to pretend again that we are "just good friends". I hate having to guard what I say all the time. Crispin, please give this some serious thought.'

'Yes I will. I'm sorry, what with Hector and everything I don't want to be a disappointment to them, but I hear you. Love you.'

'Love you too. Goodnight.'

Crispin felt a tight knot of pain and fear in his solar plexus. Was Hilary threatening to walk away? He threw himself on the bed and glanced through his wallet to check he'd transferred his euros. He saw the corner of a piece of paper at the back. His heart lurched and he slowly extracted it and re-read it for the umpteenth time.

Lieutenant Hector James Goodman MC,
Household Cavalry

Lieutenant Goodman has been posthumously awarded the Military Cross for outstanding valour. On 12th April 2011, while on foot patrol in Helmand Province, Lieutenant Goodman was leading his troops when Corporal Jason

Williams triggered an improvised explosive device and was seriously injured. Lieutenant Goodman also received extensive lacerations to his legs. The troop immediately came under small-arms fire. Lieutenant Goodman, with no thought for his own personal safety, picked up Corporal Williams to carry him to cover. At that moment Lieutenant Goodman received a bullet in the neck, killing him instantly. The rest of the platoon were safely evacuated.

Hector. Heroic, gallant, vigorous brother Hector. Three years older than Crispin and always the action man. Hector, who could make a room light up with laughter as he entered it. Hector, who won the school sports prizes and managed to get a decent-ish geography degree before joining the army. 'He died doing what he loved,' said the colonel at his funeral. Crispin gained little comfort from that and missed him terribly. Why was he on foot patrol and not in his Scimitar armoured car as per usual? He always joked that he'd joined the cavalry so he could go into battle sitting down. Hector was due to be married on his return from that tour of duty. His fiancée, Rachael, would have been a great sister-in-law but, three years later, she'd now married another officer.

Crispin bore not only his personal grief at having lost his best friend, but now carried all his mother's expectations. She had a grandchild-shaped hole in her soul and he was not sure how, or even if, he could fill it. He'd always lived in Hector's shadow and, though his parents would never have admitted it, he felt that, as an academic, he was something of a disappointment to them. If they found out about Hilary, things could get even worse.

They *did* know, after a fashion. He had managed the verbal ambiguity well enough over the last year, so that his mother, stalwart of the Mothers' Union, Women's Institute, NADFAS and the Pony Club, was still under the illusion that Hilary was a girl. Crispin's father was an archdeacon in the Oxford diocese and simply couldn't understand how 'Chaps could take up with other chaps.'

Crispin returned the cutting to its place and lay back on the bed, exhausted. This was not the first time he and Hilary had argued about his coming out to his parents and, putting himself in his partner's position, he realised he wouldn't like it much either. Could he bear to risk losing Hilary? Could he stand his parents' opprobrium?

Despite his weariness, sleep was long in coming.

CHAPTER 2

Ortigia

Thursday

After a bad night, Crispin rose early and decided to go for a run. He thought he'd take a look at the church of St John the Evangelist from the outside at least. He left the hotel, which was on a busy main road already thick with traffic, jogged to the right, past a petrol station, and right again down a pot-holed road. It was lined with modern, multi-storey residential apartments with shops on the ground floors. Some of the units were unoccupied but others looked prosperous, much the same as the apartments. Clearly the district housed a number of dogs, with poop-a-scooping not yet habitual. Crispin passed a sad little non-playing fountain, crossed a scrubby patch of grass-cum-children's play area and could now see ahead the ruins of the Byzantine church. Facing him was an end wall with an intact stone rose-window over a blocked-up neo-classical doorway. Earthquake damage had removed the roof. Along the right-hand side was an outer structure with three Romanesque arches in front of a higher wall which had once supported the roof. It housed an intricately carved doorway, above which was a roundel. The entrance to the church, which was now only a tourist site, was visible at the far end. Crispin turned and noticed the soaring spines of what resembled the concrete exoskeleton of a giant sea creature – the church of Santa Maria delle Lacrime. He jogged past the equivalent of a London Boris rent-a-bicycle stand, housing zero bikes, and around the whole

14

of Santa Maria, which was on its own roundabout. Noting the time, he sprinted back to the hotel.

Verity and Crispin breakfasted where they had dined the night before, at the top of the hotel, which also housed a small swimming pool. A fabulous spread of fruits, cereals, rolls, pastries, yoghurts, cold meats and cheese was displayed. A Gaggia coffee machine hissed in the background. From their corner table they observed that the majority of the other guests were exquisitely suited young Middle-Eastern businessmen, who appeared to be attending some conference. Mostly whippet-thin, the lines of their suits were only marred by the inevitable mobile phone collection. One glamorous woman was part of the group. Though she was dressed traditionally in a hijab, it was made of pale green silk, matching her tunic, which was edged in fine gold lacework. The only other breakfast guests were an earnest German couple, who were meticulously planning their day's sightseeing with Dorling Kindersley.

'You said your mother was Italian. How did she meet your father?' asked Crispin.

'My grandfather was a successful but mostly absent Milanese businessman, and my grandmother fulfilled the role of society hostess and charity patron. As I mentioned to Augusto, my mother, Laura, having finished school, came to Oxford to improve her English. There she fell in love with my father, a classics student called Gerald Hunter, and stayed. My grandparents were horrified, and considered that she had married beneath herself, as income from Gerald's chosen profession of schoolmaster certainly wouldn't extend to financing the ski lodges and seaside villas of her youth. However, she has always told me that she was happy in an environment of cosy stability and intellectual stimulation, rather than in the superficial *bella figura* society within which her Milanese social circle moved. I have a younger sister, Sophia, who is married with a toddler, Toby, and six-month old baby, Isabella. How about you?'

'My parents are solid middle-class Tories. I had an elder brother, Hector. He was killed in Helmand.'

'I'm so sorry. What was he like?'

'He was my hero. He was three years older than me and always on the go. Hector was both literally and metaphorically the blond-haired, blue-eyed boy. Sporty, brave, he always wanted to be a soldier and he was a fine horseman. I used to trail in his wake of glory, though he was always very protective of me, his clever-little-brother, as he often referred to me. Hector was in no way stupid, just not conventionally academic, but he was immensely practical, and a great man to have at your side in a crisis. I miss him terribly. Here.'

Crispin flicked on his phone and, scrolling down, showed Verity pictures of Hector in full dress uniform and jumping on his favourite horse.

Verity was moved. Crispin blinked rapidly and seemed to have something in his eye.

'This is my partner, Hilary,' he said, showing her another photo. 'My parents don't know I'm gay but I think they'll have to find out soon.'

She gave him a few moments to collect himself and then thought they had better turn to the matter in hand. 'I hope we can get this sightseeing trip out of the way quickly. I booked us here for a week, as I anticipated a certain amount of obfuscation, but would rather not overrun. Let's meet in the lobby just after nine to join Cesare.'

★ ★ ★

Verity was dressed in beige fitted trousers, tan loafers and her navy suit jacket, which doubled as a blazer. She had her lightweight laptop with her, which held all the accounting details and supply contracts. She hoped, forlornly, that shortly they could get to work. When Crispin arrived, he noticed small, gold initials embossed on her Radley holdall: V V T.

'What does the second V stand for?'

'Vita.'

'So, Verity Vita Hunter – truth life hunter.'

'Yes, I think they were my parent's aspirations. They weren't far wrong, though I don't know if I've been influenced by my names, or if they were just prescient. Your signet ring, is that significant?'

'My mother's family. She thinks they can trace themselves back to the Norman conquest, but not always on the right side of the blanket.'

They lapsed into comfortable silence.

Half an hour late, the black Mercedes swept up to the entrance. Cesare and Maria emerged, and Verity noted that the Merc had darkened windows and a personalised number plate.

'*Scusi, scusi Signora* Verity. Sorry to be late, I forget you English are always in time. No?'

Cesare also sported a navy blazer, his with over-large brass buttons and a lemon yellow silk lining. His white trousers, socks and shoes, coupled with a white shirt with dumbbell sized gold cufflinks, gave him a raffish, banana-republic, naval air. Maria was in tight, bright, bubble-gum pink. Cesare extravagantly kissed Verity's hand and shook Crispin's, eyeing him appraisingly. He was pretty sure he could deal with this unwelcome intrusion into his business venture, but wasn't quite certain how to read either of them – yet.

'It's very kind of you to offer to show us round, but really we're here to work and should go and see the restoration project,' protested Verity, as she was ushered into the front passenger seat. She realised as the door shut that it was unusually heavy;

bullet proof? Cesare bulldozed the car into fast-moving traffic and then caused much hooting and squealing of tyres as he executed a U-turn to head into town.

★ ★ ★

Augusto sat at his desk with his head in his hands, coffee congealing by his side. What was he to do? He had always suspected it was going to be risky giving Cesare the contract, but he had had little choice. He was obligated to Cesare. They had known each other since childhood, having been at primary school together. Augusto had always been a studious boy, and had gone on to university, first in Palermo and then to do his PhD in Naples. Cesare had grown up with his mother and five siblings, though there was some dispute about who his father actually was. His father worked on the mainland and sent money home occasionally. Cesare was a strong boy with a sharp mind, always finding ways of making money. His and Augusto's paths diverged, but Cesare had always had a soft spot for Augusto's sister, Olivia. She, however, had never wanted to marry, and lived quietly with several cats; she was the village primary school teacher.

Five years previously, Olivia had been diagnosed with an aggressive form of cancer. Having exhausted the locally available medical care, she was told that her only hope was to obtain an experimental new drug being developed in the USA. Cesare had paid for her to go to California for treatment. She survived. Augusto knew he could never repay the money, but when the restoration project came about he knew had no choice but to appoint Cesare's firm. Of course, there had been a tendering process to satisfy the Poghosian Foundation, but the result was a foregone conclusion. Augusto genuinely thought Cesare would deliver the project, if not exactly on time or within budget. However, things had not gone well. Yes, it had been more complex than they had anticipated, with rock falls in one tunnel and subsidence elsewhere, but the money seemed to get spent remarkably quickly, to little effect. Now they had found a whitewashed-over fresco. It was on a wall fairly near the entrance, suggesting an early date, as the deeper the tunnels the later the tombs.

★ ★ ★

Cesare gave a running commentary in Italian on the sights as they drove down to Ortigia.

'*Siracusa* has been populated since time out of mind. Everyone has been here. You know Archimedes, he lived here and designed ingenious war machines. During the siege of the city by the Romans in 212 BC he put up a row of polished bronze mirrors, which set ships on fire as they entered the harbour by reflecting and focusing the sun. Unfortunately, he was killed when the city was conquered, despite orders to the contrary. The story goes that he was working on mathematics and told the soldiers not to disturb him. After the Romans, the Vandals invaded, then the Goths. Things got better in the seventh century …'

An explosion of hooting erupted as Cesare jumped a red light and cut up the oncoming traffic as he approached the Foro roundabout. Grinning, he swung round Piazza Marconi and onto Via Malta.

'Yes, briefly in the seventh century, Syracuse became the capital city of the Eastern Roman Empire, but when Emperor Constans II died, that returned to Constantinople. You will see remains of Greek temples inside basilicas. Arabs entered and stayed (with a brief break) for some 190 years, being thrown out by the Normans in 1086. It is said that red-headed Sicilians, and there are many, are descended from the Normans, while the darker your skin, the more Arab your ancestors.'

Geneticists could have a field day, at the risk of political incorrectness, thought Verity.

'Later we had the Spanish, then the Austrians; even some Italians. Everybody loves to come to *Siracusa*.'

Finally, they swept over the Ponte Lucia and the old town was laid out before them. Cesare abandoned the car in front of a hotel and handed the keys and a banknote to the doorman. Cars were not allowed further into town unless you owned a property on the peninsula, as the streets were narrow and crowded. Verity suspected that this wouldn't have stopped Cesare, except that his car's paintwork might have been compromised. She noticed that all the available spaces were taken and cars had seemingly been abandoned at random, with little thought about inconveniencing the legally parked. Cesare took Verity's arm in a proprietorial manner and strode to the ruins of the sixth-century BC temple of Apollo. It had had as rumbustious a life as the city itself, having been, in turn, a Greek temple, a Byzantine church, an Arab mosque, a Norman church and a Spanish barracks, after which it had a further church built on top of it. All these additions, apart from a Norman doorway, were now stripped away, leaving several rows of Doric columns and the original floor plan. Verity found it odd to stand on the pavement with her eyes at column capital level.

Crispin and Maria followed, with Maria managing to walk remarkably well over the cobbles in her stiletto Louboutins. The language barrier condemned them to silence.

Just as Cesare was about to embark on a history of the temple, the signature tune of the children's cartoon show *Bob the Builder* emerged from his jacket. He patted his pockets, reached in and retrieved a phone. Glancing at Verity he said, 'My

grandson, he chose the aria. *Pronto. Si. Ma perche? Impossibile! …
E un castastrofo! Risolvilo! Risolvilo e basta!'*

He made a Herculean attempt to cover his agitation and
continued with their tourist trek. Turning east, they made their
way through a market with stalls bursting with produce. This
was no tourist attraction, but filled with locals haggling over
fish, some varieties of which Verity had never seen before and
appeared only to have local names. Moving on from the smell of
fish, the fragrance of warm, ripe fruit and vegetables perfumed
the air. It was crowded, but Verity noticed that people made way
for Cesare, and that many acknowledged him with respect, if
not actually with warmth. The walls of the old buildings were
festooned with phone and electricity wires. Guided through a
warren of narrow streets, they finally arrived at a magnificent
piazza, whose most striking building was the *duomo*, or cathedral.

Cesare continued his spiel as they climbed the steps to its
ornate entrance. 'This site originally housed a fifth-century BC
great temple of Athena. Here you can see the Doric columns
incorporated into a seventh-century church. Look up! The roof
of the nave is a later Norman addition. Here we have one of the
largest marble fonts you will ever see. Magnificent, no?'

Verity nodded her assent, marvelling at the style mash-up of
a building constructed over a period of twenty-three centuries.
The over-elaborate final façade was not to her taste, but she
recognised it as a striking example of the baroque.

'Here is a silver statue of Santa Lucia, our patron saint. The
entire edifice was damaged in an earthquake in the sixteenth
century and, after it was rebuilt, this wonderful baroque façade
was added in the eighteenth century by Andrea Palma, decorated
by statues carved by Ignazio Marabitti.'

As they emerged from the *duomo,* Cesare caught sight
of two *carabinieri* strolling across the piazza. He hailed them
jovially. Verity realised that these were not your normal

bobbies. One, presumably the senior, had a magnificent gold flaming grenade on his peaked cap, a braid-laden collar and epaulettes heavy with badges of rank. His companion was slightly less flamboyantly arrayed. They turned, recognised Cesare, and saluted smartly.

'*Commandante,* how delightful to encounter you!'

'*Signor Romano, che sorpresa!*'

'May I introduce *La Signora* Verity Hunter who represents the Poghosian Foundation, who are sponsoring the restoration of the catacombs, and her colleague Dr Crispin Goodman. You know Maria.'

'*Piacere, Signora, Dottore,*' they said simultaneously, while trying to tear their eyes away from Maria's décolletage.

Cesare ushered them across the piazza and through narrow streets whose two- and three-storey terraced houses sported ornate cantilevered ironwork balconies. Periodically, they had to edge past small trucks, cement mixers and piles of renovation materials, which almost blocked the roadway. Cesare continued his running commentary: the landing of Garibaldi's troops commencing the re-unification of Italy in 1848; the invasion by Allied forces in 1943; the rise of the Mafia; through to current political, economic and social issues. He paused only to point out buildings of interest, all the while staying close to Verity and occasionally touching her arm to emphasise some point. She steeled herself not to cringe and carried on smiling politely and making appropriate comments when Cesare paused for breath. As they rounded a corner he announced, 'Now lunch.'

There was no escape. It was now Thursday and Verity had hoped to have fully explored the situation for the Poghosian Foundation by the weekend as, she suspected, everything would shut down then, so that she and Crispin could compose their report and recommendations. She was clearly not in control of this situation.

'After lunch, could we go to the catacombs and start work?' she asked.

'*Certo*, of course, no problem. But first you must eat and sample some of our wonderful Sicilian dishes.' Cesare led the way down to the seafront. A wide boulevard lined with pleached trees stretched out, at the far end of which was the yacht marina. At this end was moored a single, superb motor-yacht. Verity assumed they would eat at a local restaurant nearby, but she was steered firmly towards the boat.

Cesare beamed with pride. 'My second mistress.' Verity noticed Maria wincing. *Bella Donna* was a sleek thirty metres long, with four decks including the bridge. Navy blue with crisp white markings, she looked fast and dangerous. They were greeted by members of the crew outfitted in white shorts and polo shirts embroidered *Bella Donna*. A chef, also in spotless whites, appeared on deck and bowed. On a mat by the gangplank were sets of slippers. Even Cesare removed his shoes. Verity sensed that Maria was not thrilled to lose eight centimetres in height before she was allowed on board, though presumably she was used to that.

The spotless, oiled-teak deck stretched away along the sides. In the stern was soft white leather seating curved round a teak table, which was bolted to the deck and shaded by a taut, white canopy. Stainless steel gleamed. Champagne had already been plunged into an ice bucket. In the centre of the table was a huge tureen brimful of crushed ice and containing more beluga caviar than either Verity or Crispin had ever seen, except in films. In fact, neither of them had ever eaten anything closer than lumpfish roe, which, as they were about to find out, is not at all close. That must cost hundreds of pounds, Verity thought, not realising that she was out by a factor of ten.

Cesare, with exaggerated courtesy, invited Verity to sit and then neatly trapped her against the curved seat-end. A crew member handed them hot towels. Another opened the bottle with a flourish. Vintage Bollinger. Verity thought that Cesare had misjudged how to influence British accountants when you appear to have run off with the money. She must keep sober and so must Crispin. At least Marco wasn't here to feel him up.

'Antipasto,' purred Cesare. A crew member handed around plates of blinis, heaped with caviar garnished with soured cream and slices of lemon.

'I propose a toast to a successful project.' Cesare raised his glass. '*Salute.*'

'*Salute,*' chorused the others.

'*Bella Signora* Verity, tell me about yourself. How come a beautiful woman like you is not married? You want children, no? Many men, many choices? How you come to do this finance job? What is exactly this Poghosian *Fondazione*?'

Verity felt imprisoned in her seat and again assaulted by cologne and hair-gel. She was reminded of a song from her mother's recording of the musical, *My Fair Lady*. 'Oozing charm from every pore, he oiled his way around the floor, and every trick that he could play he used to strip her mask away.'

Crispin felt for her. He knew what it was like to be interrogated about one's private life, especially if that life was not all that one had hoped for. Not that he actually knew whether Verity was contented, but he sensed she housed an inner loneliness. He took a mouthful of blini. The caviar creamed against his tongue. Smooth, with the taste of the sea. Not just salty, more complex than that, with little explosions of flavour as he burst the eggs against the roof of his mouth. It was the most delicious thing he could ever remember tasting. Now he realised why such a fuss was made about it. The champagne was in a different league from the Moët-end of the market. He was glad not to be the object of Cesare's attentions and was conscious, from her demeanour, that Maria wasn't enjoying things much at all. He realised dimly that their glasses were instantly replenished after every sip. Mustn't get drunk, he thought. I can't see much work getting done this afternoon.

A motor yacht, rather smaller than *Bella Donna*, pulled away from the marina at the far end of the boulevard and headed past them. Its horn sounded and a man in the stern waved. Cesare glanced up and waved back. 'That is the Chief Magistrate of Syracuse. He is a very good friend of mine.'

The strains of the theme tune from *Never on Sunday*, a 1950s film featuring a 'tart with a heart' sounded nearby. Immediately Cesare fumbled in his pockets for yet a third mobile, heaved himself up and went forward to take the call. Verity tried to engage Maria in conversation, but she was straining to hear what Cesare was saying. Mistress No. 1 perhaps?

'How many phones does Cesare have?' Verity asked.

'Maybe five or six. *Bob the Builder* is his cement plant and building companies. *Funiculi Funicular* is his ice-cream operation. The *Anvil Chorus* from the Verdi opera, *Il Trovatore*, is his mother, and the one with a grand tune, I don't know what it signify.'

'That waltz from Visconti's film of Lampedusa's *The Leopard*?'

Maria started and looked anxious. 'Oh that's a shipping company,' she said hurriedly. Verity didn't need to ask who the current call was from. She was impressed: she didn't think most English PAs would be familiar with opera themes, but this was Italy.

On Cesare's return, the chef announced that lunch was served. It would have been warm enough to eat on deck, but it was a little windy, so they went through the automatically opening glass doors to the saloon. Greeting them was a table caparisoned in spotless white linen and heavy silver cutlery with a forest of glasses. The auxiliary engine softly thrummed. Vintage Pouilly Fuissé was poured. Goujons of lobster cooked in a typically Sicilian sauce of onions, tomatoes, Marsala, herbs and cream, the fluffiest rice and a green salad were served. Again, their wine glasses were continually topped up. Both Verity and Crispin tried to compensate with water, but the wine was delicious. This would be a long lunch.

The silent staff wafted in and out from the galley, the chef overseeing the serving of each course. Slivers of pink veal served with lemon, capers and sautéed zucchini were accompanied by fine claret. Then came zabaglione, an exquisite creamy concoction of beaten eggs and Marsala, light, tangy, caressing the tongue. Vintage Vin Santo and almond biscotti accompanied coffee.

'Signora Verity, is it possible show you my *Bella Donna*?'

'Thank you. That would be lovely.' Verity found she could barely stand and felt very sleepy.

Cesare ushered her up the companionway to the bridge, which had a commanding view of the port. A few sailing yachts were out and a tourist boat, in the shape of an old-fashioned wooden pirate ship, was setting off for a tour of nearby coves and islands. The sky held a few clouds, more for artistic effect than rain potential, and the sea glittered, reflecting the blue of the sky. The town stretched up the hill behind them. The helmsman's white leather swivel-seat was bolted to the deck. The cockpit had an array of screens, radar, GPS, depth sounder, dials showing air pressure, wind speed and direction, engine revs and temperature, a radio, fuel gauges and others, the purpose of all of which was unclear to Verity. The wheel and the controls for the huge twin engines commanded the display. To one side there was a chart table, paper charts and a magnetic compass on gimbals, only to be used in the unlikely event of all the electronics going down.

'She is very fast, top speed of thirty-five knots and she travel 325 nautical miles before she need gas. Tell me how much you think one tank of fuel costs?'

'I have no idea.'

'Try.'

'No really, I have no idea.'

'Five thousand euro!' he trumpeted. 'Come and see the rest of her.' He led the way down the stairs into the saloon where Crispin and Maria still sat, absorbed in their own thoughts. Through the glass doors they saw the captain arriving. He was attired in a spotless white uniform topped by a peaked cap sporting sufficient gold braid for a Latin-American admiral. He greeted Maria, had a word with one of the crew and then offered to show Crispin the bridge. Cesare ignored him and led Verity down a corridor.

Cesare opened the door to the first cabin on the port side and ushered Verity in. Along one wall were mirrored, fitted wardrobes, ending with a mirror-backed dressing table. Opposite was a large double bed with a deep purple and gold silk coverlet adorned by lime-green scatter cushions topped by a padded, gilded headboard. The upholstery and cushions on the two armchairs were in the same colours, reversed. Gilded *putti* sidelights and a Swarovski chandelier completed the décor. Verity kept a straight face and wondered what the English Heritage style-police would make of it.

'*Tremendo,* no? You like it?'

'It's very luxurious.'

He opened a door into the bathroom. Here at least the upholsterers had not been given free rein. All was white Carrara marble, apart from the gold, dolphin-shaped taps. Purple and lime-green towels completed the ensemble. Crossing the corridor, Cesare entered another cabin, standing just inside the doorway so Verity had to squeeze past. His hand skimmed her back but she deftly avoided its intended trajectory. Electric blue was the theme colour with orange accents, which clashed with the gilt.

'I am sure you must have a secret boyfriend, a beautiful woman like you. Is he married or famous?'

As he said this, Cesare stepped closer and Verity began to feel increasingly uncomfortable, but slapped down her instincts, not believing anyone could be so brazen. She swerved, employing some neat choreography to avoid close contact, but the tour was not yet over. Cesare ushered her further along the corridor, past several other cabins, to the one at the end.

'Master suite.' He opened the door with a flourish, stepped aside and Verity entered with faint foreboding. Oh, don't be silly, she thought, he wouldn't be so stupid as to make a pass at me. Here crimson replaced the purple with shocking pink accents and even more gold. Verity heard the door shut and click; her ears were assailed by some loud, thumping music. The next moment Cesare was up behind her, having shed his jacket. He pressed her against the raised leather padded foot of the circular bed, wrapped his left arm around hers and started roughly fondling her right breast. He kissed her ear and neck urgently, his hot boozy breath almost suffocating her, while his right hand went between her thighs.

'Stop it, NO NO!' she shouted, struggling ineffectually. His weight controlled her.

'No one can hear you and they wouldn't disturb us if they could.'

Verity tried to slip her right hand between her legs to grab him but he had trapped her. She could feel his erection hard against her back. He undid her trousers with a practised hand, pulled them down and bent her face-down over the bed, spreading her legs with his own. She strained, almost suffocating in the coverlet. Beyond the beat of the music, the strains of a waltz sounded. Cesare hesitated. That phone never rang unless it was urgent. Verity seized her chance. She thrust her hand between her legs, grabbed his groin, twisted and squeezed. He grunted and stumbled backwards. Verity turned, shoved him off balance, dragged up her trousers and fled. She staggered into one of the cabins and locked the door. Collapsing in the bathroom, she retched into the loo. Caviar, lobster, veal, pudding, wine, the lot came up. Gradually she recovered herself. Her shirt was speckled with vomit. Her countenance was grey. She straightened out her clothes as best she could, rinsed her mouth, listened carefully at the door, then sprinted out into the saloon. Crispin and the captain looked up startled. Maria had disappeared.

'Verity, are you all right, what's happened?'

'Get us out of here,' she croaked.

'Call us a taxi for the hotel,' Crispin demanded, 'now.'

The Captain was under no illusion as to what had happened but he dare not obey without his boss's consent.

'*Momento.*'

He disappeared in the direction of the master suite and swiftly returned.

'*Il Signore* says sorry not to see you off, he has some urgent business.' He flicked out his mobile and moments later they saw a taxi peel off the marina rank and drive the length of the quay to the ship.

'Hotel Hermes *versus theatrum Graecum,*' managed Crispin, as he helped Verity into the front seat. Smelling vomit, the taxi driver looked concerned that more might be on its way, but Crispin assured him in Italian-accented Latin that it would be OK.

Holding herself rigid and staring straight ahead Verity got as far as her room but couldn't insert the keycard with her shaking hand. Crispin gently took it from her and ushered her in. She collapsed on the bed and shock set in. Crispin covered her with the duvet and got water from the minibar.

'Would you like me to get a doctor?'

'No, no, I'm all right really,' she said through chattering teeth.

'Verity, I really think I should call the police.'

'No, nothing happened.'

'Obviously something happened; you've been seriously assaulted at the very least. Are you sure you don't want a doctor? You don't look at all good.'

'No, please, really, I'll be all right in a bit.'

Crispin sat next to the window and waited. Gradually her trembling subsided and some colour returned to her face.

'Shall I get in touch with the office and arrange for you to fly home? There must be someone else who can do this?'

'No Crispin, please. I was stupid. I should never have allowed myself to get into such a vulnerable position. I'll be fine. Worse things happen at sea.'

'We were at sea.'

She smiled weakly.

'I can't do anything this afternoon, but please phone Augusto, saying we will be at his office first thing tomorrow and will countenance no more delays. Cesare is not to be there.'

'Only if you're sure. Can I order you anything from room service?'

'No thanks, I'll be better after I've slept. I'm sorry to be like this. Will you be OK alone this evening?'

'Verity don't be silly, of course I'll be OK. I might even do a bit more sightseeing at this end of town. You can always get me on my mobile.'

'Please ring Augusto, and I'll see you in the morning.'

'Consider it done. Shall we meet again at eight for breakfast?'

Verity nodded her assent and managed another weak smile, despite the wave of nausea induced by the word breakfast.

Crispin went next door and picked up the phone. Marco answered it, and was delighted to hear Crispin, who cut him short and demanded to speak to *Il Direttore*.

After a bit Verity picked up her mobile and speed-dialled her sister.

'Hi V, how's Sicily?'

'Oh Sophie, I feel such a fool.'

Why, what's happened? You sound terrible.'

Verity recounted the events on the yacht.

'V, how dreadful! Are you sure you're OK physically? Shouldn't you see a doctor? What about the police? Has Crispin called them?'

No, I wouldn't let him. Our Sicilian friend seems to have the heads of both the police and judiciary in his pocket. Who'd believe me? Anyhow, I'm only shocked, but I don't know how I'm going to face that man again. He gave me the creeps right from the start.'

'Perhaps he'll keep his distance,' Sophie offered. 'I'm so sorry. Try and get some sleep. I'll pray for you.'

'Much good *that* will do.'

'Well you never know, and prayer has no known adverse side-effects.'

'Thanks Soph, I'll need all the help I can get with this job. Fortunately Crispin is a really decent bloke and we work well together.'

'Romantic prospect?'

'No. Not camp as a row of tents exactly, but definitely gay.'

'You're sounding a bit better already. Sorry, I have to go. We're having a bit of a toddler tantrum this end. But you can always ring me. You know that.'

'Thanks Soph. I feel much better already. Please don't tell anyone about this.'

'Shan't breathe a word. Lots of love. Bye.'

'Bye Soph. Thanks. Speak to you soon.'

Verity lay back and went over and over the events of the day. Eventually she slept.

CHAPTER 3

St John the Evangelist

Friday

Verity and Crispin walked the route of Crispin's earlier run, past the petrol station, round the corner, down the potholed road flanked by apartment blocks, across the sad little children's play area and into the entrance of the Pontificia Commissione di Archeologia: Sacra Catacomb di San Giovanni, as stated on a brass plaque at the gate. A beautiful, well-tended garden with mature trees and exotic plants greeted them. Gravel paths wound their way to the front of an impressive eighteenth-century style villa. Marco had been keeping an eye out for them and came down the steps as they approached. This time, he made an effort to be civil to Verity, while surreptitiously winking at Crispin.

Augusto's first-floor office was high-ceilinged and spacious, facing onto the gardens. His antique desk was topped by a computer screen and teetering piles of papers. The herringbone parquet floor was partially covered by a handsome Turkish rug. Translucent roller-blinds partially shrouded the windows, which were flanked by burgundy velvet curtains restrained by thick silky ropes. A chandelier added to the grandeur. Marring the opulence were several battleship-grey steel filing cabinets ranged along one wall. Away from the desk was a table on which the plans of the catacombs and its proposed renovations were laid out, along with the claimed progress reports, cash-flows and a pile of invoices, most of which were from Cesare.

Augusto rose from his desk and came forward to greet them. He introduced Cesare's site supervisor, Volpe, a short, red-headed, sharp-faced man who, after introductions and the interruption caused by the arrival of espressos, launched into an explanation of what had happened thus far. He spoke rapid Italian, with a strong Sicilian accent, to follow which required all of Verity's concentration. Crispin rapidly realised it was far too fast for his Latin translation trick, so he tuned out, turning his attention to the plans, which included the areas where rock falls were supposed to have happened. He was surprised, as there had been no historical record of any such misfortune. Augusto looked on anxiously. Marco bided his time.

Having absorbed most of what Volpe had explained, Verity extracted her laptop, opened the budget spreadsheets, and demonstrated the rapid divergence of the planned and actual cash expenditure, with seemingly little progress on the ground. Volpe waved the invoices at her, insisting that they were all countersigned by *Il Direttore* and all justified.

Verity sensed what accountants call a 'snow-job': instead of concealing key information, it is swamped by so much data that, in a limited time period, it is almost impossible to unearth it. Consequently, she cut Volpe short.

'I will take all of these, if I may, and study them in my own time,' she announced to Augusto. He nodded wordlessly. Verity was again aware of his discomfort. He knows he has got himself into a tight hole, she thought. I wonder what Cesare has on him?

The morning wore on as they studied the drawings and figures and debated a plan of action. Verity was becoming beside herself with frustration at not being able to see the actual site. Then Augusto said, 'Forgive me but I have a long-standing lunch engagement. I know you are keen to survey the catacombs. So, shall we meet at the entrance to the church at two-thirty? The foreman, Giuseppe, will accompany us.'

'Fine,' said Verity. She gathered up the invoices and her laptop and she and Crispin wandered round the corner to Café Mauro where they had panini. It was warm enough to sit outside, so they had a good view of the soaring big-top-like dome of the church of Madonna delle Lacrime. Its grounds were planted with palm trees, softening the look of the roundabout. Ambulances with sirens blaring passed at regular intervals as the local hospital was just down the road. Two young mothers pushing baby buggies each containing a couple of children came and sat at a nearby table. They busied themselves with the paraphernalia for feeding the two babies and settling their toddlers in high chairs while the waitress took their order. Both Verity and Crispin looked over fondly. Verity was reminded of her nephew and niece and Crispin wondered again if he could ever be a father. He loved kids and they responded well to him.

Augusto managed unusually to be on time for once and he and Marco ushered them into the spartan entrance hall, which was intended to become a more informative visitors' centre. A couple of bored-looking staff, who usually sold tickets and guide books, had little to do as the church closed, but they made an effort to look busy when they recognised Augusto. A ginger kitten had moved in, looking imperiously at them from the base of an elaborately engraved sarcophagus. It reminded Crispin of Tarquin, his mog at home. Above ground was a ruined mash-up of Greek temple doorways and columns, incorporated into a Byzantine church. The building was open to the sky following earthquake damage. This edifice had been built over a chapel where the theologian Marcion had been buried, at least for a time, and it was reputed to be the place of his martyrdom in AD 160. Marcion had thought that the God of the Old Testament was an evil demiurge and had nothing to do with the God of the New Testament, so he had tried to remove all Old Testament references from the New Testament, leaving it somewhat sparse. His approach was subsequently denounced by the Church as a heresy.

Augusto, Marco, Verity, Crispin and Giuseppe entered the subterranean church down wide stone steps leading into a cellar-like cavern with various vaulted side-rooms. Verity looked around her. Augusto started to describe what they were seeing and to identify the frescos of various saints. He then led them over to a rough stone block altar in front of a small curved apse on which was a damaged depiction of St Paul.

'This is said to be where St Paul preached and announced the Gospel of Jesus Christ when he came to Syracuse. Obviously, it was not in a church building at the time, but was above the Greek water-storage cisterns. They were subsequently converted into catacombs. Shall we go on?'

Augusto led them to the entrance, where there was a plan of the catacombs on the wall. It showed a long, straight corridor off which some dozen smaller galleries branched at ninety degrees. These in turn were extended into a network linking several circular caverns at each side of the main corridor. The galleries were lined with hollowed-out tunnels, which had been packed with sarcophagi over centuries.

Augusto pointed to the entrance. 'We are here. These catacombs are very extensive as you can see. In fact they cover some 10,000 square metres, similar to a football pitch. Most of what we have here dates from the fourth century, following earlier earthquake damage. The original plan was that of the Greek water cisterns and their connecting tunnels. That is what those circular shapes are. You will see that they are spacious domes extending up to the surface. The rock here is soft limestone, so is relatively easy to excavate.'

'Would the oldest burials be near this entrance with younger ones deeper in?' asked Verity.

'Exactly! Up to thirty bodies were found in some tombs. They would appear to be from extended families. The tomb tunnels are sufficiently wide that they could continue to excavate more deeply beyond the existing bodies. You will also see niches in all the galleries where single persons were laid, often in a neonatal position, ready for new birth at the resurrection. When considered complete, the tomb entrances were often sealed up, sometimes with terracotta, on which were painted frescos.'

Verity was itching to get into the catacombs; however Augusto's academic enthusiasm could not be curtailed.

★ ★ ★

Maria applied her make-up carefully. She had a sultry southern beauty and oozed sex appeal. However, she was no fool. She had come a long way from her impoverished beginnings and was determined never to return. One of seven children, she was bright but had had little chance of a decent formal education. She had been determined to better herself and from a young age she washed dishes at the local internet cafe in return for computer time. Seeing she was keen, her primary-school teacher taught her the rudiments of touch typing. On the internet, she enrolled on accounting and commercial courses. Reading voraciously, she actively extended her vocabulary and grasp of grammar. Graduating to serve in the local bar, she discovered that her good looks and voluptuous figure were a hit with the customers. She could make men salivate at will; good for tips. Disdaining the advances of the local lads, she consciously avoided the trap of an early marriage and endless children.

Meeting Cesare had been her big chance. Financing a

daytime secretarial course in Syracuse by acting as a nightclub 'escort', she had caught his eye as he swaggered up to the bar. He had come with a lady friend.

He left with Maria.

They made a good team. As Cesare grew to trust her, and as his business affairs increased in complexity and scale, he allowed Maria greater autonomy over handling some of his shadier financial dealings. Volpe did the official and unofficial tax returns and 'bought off' officials and the opposition, whereas Maria handled some interesting cash flows through a myriad of offshore accounts. She had excelled herself by mastering the convoluted manoeuvrings required for an asset swap of cement plants with a minor Russian oligarch. As a reward, while Cesare was still on a high over the deal, she persuaded him to put her name on the title deeds of the very smart apartment in which he had set her up.

She glanced out of its picture window onto the bay. In the underground garage sat her scarlet Alfa Romeo, Giulietta. But Maria was worried. Not everything had been going brilliantly. Cesare's wife and family were no problem, but that new mobile phone could only mean one of two things: either he had a new business of which she knew nothing, or a new mistress. Suspecting the latter, she felt a frisson of fear. A flat and a car were all very well and Cesare paid her generously, but that could stop in an instant. Maria was determined to secure her lifestyle before anything went wrong. In anticipation of this day, she had opened bank accounts in Luxemburg and the Cayman Islands. This was easily done as the paperwork piggybacked on accounts she had set up for Cesare. Now she must work on how to siphon money into them without being noticed. The 'shipping' profits were the hardest to trace. She would start with those.

'Shipping' was how she had referred to the Lampedusa

ringtone, on Verity's enquiry. 'People trafficking' would have been a more accurate description. It was hard to imagine a more lucrative venture. Great wedges of untraceable cash were passed on by hand through code-named middlemen, with the sailors and ripped-off refugees running all the risks.

CHAPTER 4

The bronze-bound chest

Friday

Giuseppe, Verity and Crispin walked down the tomb tunnel in which the hidden fresco had been found. The passage was not much shorter than the others, so its end wall had not attracted attention for centuries. The fresco had been effectively camouflaged by rendering it with rough plaster which had been painted to resemble the surrounding walls. A large sarcophagus had blocked the end, to discourage any extension of the tunnel. The fresco had only been discovered when the sarcophagus was removed for renovation and some of the render had fallen away. The rest was being painstakingly removed and the feet and robes of a man were emerging from the bottom right-hand corner. This tunnel, like the others, was lit by a single strand of wiring, some of it bare, connecting precariously positioned light bulbs, draped along a wall. Crispin supplemented this light by wearing a head-torch he normally used when cycling. Giuseppe demonstrated his method of removing the render. Crispin was slightly concerned at the use of a sharp trowel. Giuseppe detached a hand-sized piece from the underlying plaster. As he leant towards the wall, he unaccountably toppled forward, put an arm out to save himself and, to everyone's horror, pushed a large section of plaster into the gap beyond it.

The wall was false. With a howl of prayers to the Madonna, and muttering about *Il Direttore*, and his job, Giuseppe fled back down the tunnel, leaving Verity and Crispin to view the damage.

'Why couldn't they tell it was hollow?' Verity queried.

'I don't suppose they'd tapped it.' Peering at the broken edge with the help of his head-torch, Crispin said, 'It seems to have been backed onto narrow bricks and the mortar has crumbled, hence the collapse.'

'Can we move the broken piece?'

'We probably should leave it, but I don't suppose we'll do it any more harm.'

The broken plaster section was about the size of a manhole cover. Crispin carefully slid the trowel under its nearest side, leaned in, gently folded his fingertips under its far edge, and gingerly pulled the piece back though the hole. They slid the plaster onto a discarded *Giornale di Sicilia* newspaper and placed it to one side. Crispin poked his head through the hole and looked around. The tunnel continued briefly, ending in a roughly cut limestone wall. Without analysing why, Crispin found himself crawling through the hole. Turning, he could see that indeed much of the mortar had separated from the thin Roman bricks, leaving an unstable support for the plaster front. As he touched a section, it fell away into his hand. He thought that instead of removing the render from the front, perhaps the entire edifice should be stabilised at its back as, he suspected, it was the render that was holding much of the structure together. Scanning the rest of the small space before leaving, he froze. His light had caught the dull reflection of metal on what appeared to be a chest, fitted into a waist-high niche.

'Verity, you've got to see this!'

'What is it?'

'Just look,' he said, extracting himself carefully from the hole. Verity fumbled in her bag, finding a small torch and directing it towards where Crispin indicated. On seeing the chest, she inched her way through the hole and stood up carefully. Crispin followed. He turned to her, blinding her with his torch.

'Sorry.'

They gazed at a bronze-bound wooden chest supported by bossed feet in the shape of lion paws. It was covered in a thin film of limestone dust. There were handles at each end and it was similar in size to a case of wine. Both knew that they should wait for archaeologists to inspect and examine the chest in situ but the temptation was too great. Verity attempted to lift the lid, to no avail. There was an elaborate-looking lock on the front. She glanced either side and then peered underneath it. Her sneeze disturbed some dust and she saw what looked like a bulge. It was too far back for her to reach.

'What do we have that could get to what might be the key?' she asked. They both thought through the contents of their bags, which were sitting on the other side of the hole.

'I suppose some rolled-up paper might do.' Verity crouched down and could just reach her bag. She pulled out a wodge of Cesare's invoices. With a wry smile she rolled some sheets tightly together and managed to edge the key, for that was what it was, to where her outstretched fingers could reach it. She inserted it into the lock and tried to turn it, to no avail. It was solid both ways. She wiggled it around, this way and that.

'You don't happen to have any WD-40 in that bag of yours?'

'Funnily enough, no.'

Verity continued to fiddle and then, with no warning, the key turned. She attempted to lift the lid, but it seemed stuck. Crispin had a go and it creaked open, its unexpected weight explained by a lead lining.

'That should have kept the contents intact,' he commented.

The first thing they could see was a linen cloth, which Verity carefully folded back, revealing a single papyrus sheet. Breaking all the conservation rules, she picked it up. The lead had preserved it perfectly. Written along its length in Greek script was:

To Reuben, Elizabeth and all the Saints in the church in Syracuse, from Timothy, Apostle to our Lord Christ Jesus. Greetings.

Both of them gasped and looked at each other, Crispin's light blinding Verity once more. She said, 'Do you realise no one has read this since the first century? It's amazing!' She turned it over and they both began to read. It was a struggle, as there were no gaps between the words. After a couple of sentences she commented, 'The Greek looks a bit odd to me.'

'It's Koine Greek,' Crispin responded, 'which was used all over the Near East in the first century. It's a simplified and regularised form of the classical language which you will have studied. The New Testament is written in it. One of the best arguments for dumbing-down I've ever encountered.'

Voices could be heard at a distance and they both paused, but no one came. Giuseppe was probably playing for time before he admitted the damage he had caused, but they might not be private for much longer. Crispin translated

I am sending you this casket for safekeeping. It contains letters received by our dear brother Paul, along with some of his effects, as I know you love him well. I hope to join you later in the year. The sea captain to whom I have entrusted this casket is in the Way.

You may have heard by now that our dear bother Paul was martyred on the orders of the Emperor Nero for blasphemy and sedition. He would not worship His Imperial Majesty as a god and had caused the Synagogue in Jerusalem to denounce him. He was beheaded by a sword on the Appian Way, as befits a Roman citizen. On the same day, our beloved brother Peter was executed on identical charges. He, who had known our Lord Jesus Christ personally and shared his ministry, was crucified. He refused to be hanged as his Lord had been, so they nailed him upside-down. He took several days to die. Peter was one of our church leaders in Jerusalem and the one of whom Jesus had said that he would be 'the rock on which his church would be built and against which Hell could not prevail'. All of us are in fear for our lives but we trust in our Lord to bring us to safety or to give us the courage to face a martyr's death with confidence. We have a sure and certain hope of eternal life though the death and resurrection of our Lord Christ Jesus.

May the Lord bless you and your households.

Your brother in Christ, Timothy

'This is dynamite!' Verity gasped.

'Verity, we really should get Augusto to see these now.'

'If we do, we may never have a chance to look at them again. You know how secretive and controlling the Vatican is. Kairós works for a papal organisation after all.'

Verity folded back another layer of linen revealing numerous scrolls of papyri. There seemed to be four sets of slightly different widths and differing quality. The scrolls had dried out too much to be able to unroll them. They would have to reintroduce some humidity, which couldn't be done there. Verity had spent a summer at the University of Michigan, in Ann Arbor, on a conservation course specialising in papyrus. It had one of the world's finest collections. She felt confident that she could unroll the scrolls without damage, provided she had time and access to steam. Both she and Crispin were more than conscious that they should only be handling these texts in controlled climatic conditions wearing cotton gloves, not in a dusty tunnel with sweaty hands. However, it was far too exciting to stop and, as Verity pointed out, they might never have another opportunity.

Of course unrolling them would only be the first step. Documents were written using only capital letters (lower case having not been developed until a later period) but with no gaps between the words and no punctuation. As Greek used word-endings to denote the verb tense and role played by nouns and adjectives and so on, this style of presentation produced less ambiguity than might be supposed at first sight. However, to translate, first it would be necessary to transcribe the text, dividing up the words and inserting some modern punctuation for clarity. It would not be a quick process.

With trembling fingers, Crispin extracted a long scroll of papyrus, noting its original position. The outside surface was inscribed along the horizontal fibres of the sheet. The back of each sheet had the fibres laid at ninety degrees to the writing surface to give strength, but would have been hard to write on, as quill nibs tended to catch in the fibres, spattering ink.

From Rabbi Gamaliel in Jerusalem to Marcus Antonius
Paulus (also known as Saul) in Caesarea. Greetings.

Verity thought she was going to faint, and not just because the air quality was poor. The name Gamaliel rang a faint bell with her; wasn't he mentioned somewhere in the New Testament? She said, 'I can't bear the thought of us not seeing these first. This has got be more exciting than whatever post-doc research you're doing.'

'Er yes, but how can we? We can't just steal them.'

'No, but we could *borrow* them,' ventured Verity. 'No one knows they're here, the office and the renovation work are about to shut down for the weekend. The catacombs have been closed to the public under that coverall phrase beloved of Italian churches and museums *Chiuso, sotto restauro,* with no suggestion of how long before they'll open again. We could just take the scrolls for the weekend and return them before anyone finds out. I don't trust the Vatican not to suppress these as soon as they hear about them. Augusto will have to contact the papal authorities in Rome, and they, no doubt, will whisk some cardinal down here to take them into custody for "study and safekeeping". That may be the last we and the world ever see of them.'

It was a crazy suggestion, totally unprofessional, but they might just get away with it. Verity hadn't thought clearly how they were going to return the scrolls to the chest without others being present, but that would be Monday's problem.

She urged, 'Between us we can probably put them in our bags, lock the chest and take the key. Then, though Giuseppe and the others will see the chest, they won't dare move it and it will look untouched.'

'Verity, if we get caught we could go to prison for ages,' Crispin objected. 'Stealing Italian, not to say religious, treasures, is considered a heinous crime and both our careers would be ruined. Pre-trial incarceration could last years. Look at Amanda Knox and Raffaele Sollecito who were held for months after her flatmate was found stabbed in Perugia.'

'We won't be being accused of murder. Anyhow, why should they catch us?'

Verity felt light-headed. She had always 'kicked against the pricks' and had a well-developed ability to argue herself out of trouble later. This was a once-in-a-lifetime opportunity to look at something original before anyone else did, and who knew what historical secrets the letters might contain? Though she had lost her religious faith long ago, her heart had burned slightly as she handled the letter from Gamaliel.

Faint sounds of distant shouting could be heard. It was now or never. Verity looked at Crispin and got another eyeful of light.

'Well?' she challenged him.

Crispin took a big breath. 'OK let's do it, but God help us if this goes wrong.'

Verity crawled back through the hole and Crispin handed her the scrolls one at a time. She placed two sets in his bag and the rest in hers.

'There's something else. It feels like a metal plate in a black fabric case. It's not linen. Oh my God!'

'What is it?'

'The fabric is disintegrating as I look at it. It must be the reaction with the air. That happened to the feather fans in Tutankhamun's tomb. Howard Carter photographed them and after a few minutes they crumbled into dust. They'll know we've opened this now.'

'Not necessarily, it could have happened while sealed up. You said there was a metal plate?'

'Yes, actually I think it's two, ring-hinged and sealed together. It looks like bronze, though it's hard to see in this light. It seems to have inscriptions on the back and front.'

'Let's have that as well. May as well be hung for a sheep as a lamb.'

Crispin felt that he himself was a lamb being led to the slaughter. No going back now. He locked the chest and pocketed the key, then inched his way back through the hole.

'We'd better tell them about the chest, as they'll see our footprints in the dust.'

At that moment, voices could be heard bursting with Mediterranean hysteria. Augusto, Marco and Giuseppe careered into the tunnel, their bobbing heads throwing jumping shadows onto the walls. Verity and Crispin were preternaturally calm and desperately trying not to look guilty. Augusto saw the hole.

'*Oddio mio!* It's a disaster! You stupid, clumsy idiot!'

'I think it can be repaired, but we've found something amazing that would never have been discovered if Giuseppe hadn't slipped,' said Verity.

Augusto examined the broken piece and the hole and then, with the aid of Verity's torch, peered though and saw the chest.

'*Oddio mio! Madonna!* What is here? Have you looked at it?'

'Yes. It seemed very heavy so we thought we should leave it,' said Verity, feeling as though the papyri were burning a hole through her case.

After a certain amount of arguing in rapid Sicilian, none of which Verity could understand, Augusto turned to her and Crispin and said in borken English, 'Now is too late to bring the archaeologist from the University of Palermo. He come next week. The catacombs we must close with key. I telephone Palermo.'

At the word *key*, Crispin twitched and perspiration trickled down his back. He felt nauseous and hoped no one would notice.

'Well if you're sure,' said Verity, 'but don't be too hard on Giuseppe.'

Augusto threw his eyes up to heaven, but realised that it had been a lucky break, in every sense. They trooped out, with Verity and Crispin on tenterhooks, desperate to get away.

'Let's go back to the office,' Augusto invited.

Verity could think of no plausible reason to refuse. She followed Augusto.

Marco and Crispin hung back a bit, and she heard them murmuring. She suspected Marco could speak more English than he had let on. Giuseppe locked up and slunk away.

It took a while to establish that there was no one left in

the University of Palermo's Department of Archaeology so late on a Friday afternoon, so Augusto sent an email copying in Verity for the reply. Naples University was the regional centre of excellence for papyri, but Augusto wanted to keep things Sicilian for as long as possible.

'Stay for an *aperitivo*. I insist!' Augusto turned and extracted a bottle of Sicilian white wine from his office fridge and poured four glasses. He was in a quandary. This find could perhaps improve the situation he found himself in, with so little to show for the money that had thus far been spent. He desperately wanted to get Verity and Crispin onside, but had heard that some unfortunate incident had occurred on Cesare's yacht; the taxi driver was a cousin of the office's gardener.

'Forgive me for not entertaining you this weekend, but it is my mother's eightieth birthday and we have a big family party back in our village. You know that Monday is *festa* and everything will be closed. We celebrate Santa Cecilia of Syracuse. The Church has moved her official saint's day but now we just celebrate two times.'

'Oh that's fine,' said Verity, 'we have work to do and can amuse ourselves.'

Eventually, they escaped and made it back to the hotel. On the way, they passed a pharmacy, which sold them a pack of surgical gloves. Verity motioned Crispin into her room and carefully extracted her scrolls, laying them out on the bed. She put on the kettle and Crispin went and brought his in. She also ran the shower, attempting to fill the bathroom with steam, though the air extractor was a bit more efficient than she would have liked.

'Before we start work, Crispin, can you remember the order they were arranged in the chest, as we'd better make a note of it?'

'Yes I think so,' he replied. 'They were grouped together

with the smaller scrolls on the top left, next to them, Gamaliel and then these two. Let's see who they're from.'

From Barnabas in Cyprus to Marcus Antonius Paulus in Antioch. Greetings

From Prisca wife of Aquila in Ephesus to Marcus Antonius Paulus in Jerusalem. Greetings

'Good heavens! This is amazing! Barnabas and Prisca. It can't be surely?' Crispin exclaimed.

'Why? Do you know who they are?' asked Verity.

'If indeed they're the same people, according to the Acts of the Apostles, Barnabas was a colleague of Paul and accompanied him on many of his missionary journeys. They fell out big time over Barnabas wanting to take John Mark with them and Paul objecting, as he had abandoned them once before. Paul and Barnabas split up, Barnabas travelling with John Mark to Cyprus and Paul going on to Syria and Cilicia. According to Church tradition, John Mark is the author of Mark's Gospel, which he took down as dictation from the apostle Peter, possibly translating from Aramaic to Greek as he wrote. If you read it in the original Greek, you can see Semitic idioms coming through at times, which, at least to me, makes that theory plausible. Tradition also has it that Jesus' last supper was held in John Mark's family's house in Jerusalem. That would imply they were wealthy, as to have an upper room which could hold a minimum of thirteen diners – there were probably more of them present, plus the servants – would require one to be well-off.'

'How do you know all this?' asked Verity.

'My father is an archdeacon and I have attended church every Sunday for forever.'

'Do you believe in God, Jesus as his son and all that?'

'Yes I do. I lost my faith for a while as a teenager, and only went to church under protest. Somehow God got me again. It's a strange and wonderful thing. How about you?'

'My mother brought me up as a Catholic, but by the time I was fourteen it all seemed so implausible and the Church's teaching on so many things was so unacceptable, that I gave the whole thing up. Paedophile priests and their conniving cardinals didn't exactly help either. I'd like to believe, but I just can't. I envy you.'

'You know that amazing-looking pointed roof we see from the catacomb entrance? It's Santa Maria delle Lacrime, St Mary of the Tears. I jogged round it on Friday, and thought I might go there on Sunday. Would you like to come?'

'I'll think about it. Let's look at this last batch. Hang on, I can't read this, it's not in Greek. It looks like a funny sort of Hebrew. Does it make any sense to you?' She handed the first scroll over.

Crispin squinted at the writing. Initially puzzled, he then exclaimed, 'It's in Aramaic. I did a bit with Syriac as part of my degree. Mind you, it's pretty rusty and what with this flamboyant handwriting, transcribing it will be time consuming. Painfully he made out:

From Bernice, widow of Marcus Antonius Lucius residing in Tarsus, to Marcus Antonius Paulus in Corinth, Greetings.

'Who's she?'

'I've no idea. We'll have to unroll it.'

By now, the bathroom was as steamy as it was going to get and they carefully laid the tightly rolled scrolls on every available horizontal surface. Crispin gingerly held the Bernice letter over a steaming kettle, trying not to scald his hand or get the papyrus too wet. All the while the kettle kept switching itself off.

'I noticed a cooking utensils shop round the corner,' said Verity. 'If they're open tomorrow perhaps we should buy some oven gloves and tongs? A less than usual expense account item.'

Crispin grinned and, sensing the papyrus relaxing, laid it down on a face towel. Glancing at Verity and holding his breath, he gingerly unrolled it.

He picked out the first and last sentences to see if they could provide a clue as to the sender.

My Darling Sauli

Your worrying and loving Mama, Bernice

Crispin almost dropped the letter in his excitement. 'If these are from Paul's mother, we'll learn things about Paul that no one's ever known before! This is just sensational!' He looked up in wonder at Verity. In some ways she reminded him of Hector, fearless, adventurous and resourceful, though Verity was clearly muh cleverer academically than his brother. Despite the risks they were taking, he somehow felt safe with her. 'A good one to have at your side in a crisis,' as Hector would have said. Although, despite Verity's outward resilience, Crispin had detected a seam of loneliness. He was so grateful for Hilary.

'Let's look at this bronze plaque first,' suggested Verity. 'You said it was inscribed.'

SPQR

This is to certify that Marcus Antonius Paulus is a citizen of the Roman Republic. He is the son of Marcus Antonius Lucius and grandson of Marcus Antonius Saulus, of Tarsus, who gave great assistance to Triumvir Marcus Antonius and the Republic in supplying his army with tents. For this service, he and his descendants were granted citizenship in perpetuity, in the year of the Roman Consuls Sextus Pomius and Lucius Cornificius. Let this be known.

On the back were inscribed the names of seven witnesses, their bronze seals hanging from linen ribbons clamped within the sealed plates.

Verity glanced at her watch. 'Let's put *Do not disturb* on the doors and get a bit of dinner. I noticed a nice looking trattoria not far from here. I find hotel restaurants a bit soulless. Then perhaps we can start to unroll the others. Tomorrow we can study these and confer. I'll take photos of everything and email them to each of us, so we have a record.'

They divided the documents up, with Crispin taking half of Gamaliel's and the Aramaic ones, leaving Verity the ones written in Greek.

On her return from dinner, Verity showered and washed her hair. In searching for the hairdryer she opened a drawer and found it along with a Bible placed there by the Gideon Society. Idly she flicked through it and it fell open at Acts of the Apostles 28:1.

Once safely on shore, we found out that the island was called Malta. The islanders showed us unusual kindness. They built a fire and welcomed us all because it was raining and cold. Paul gathered a pile of brushwood and, as he put it on the fire, a viper, driven out by the heat, fastened itself on his hand. When the islanders saw the snake hanging from his hand, they said to each other, 'This man must be a murderer; for though he escaped from the sea, Justice has not allowed him to live.' But Paul shook the snake off into the fire and suffered no ill effects. The people expected him to swell up or suddenly fall dead, but after waiting a long time and seeing nothing unusual happen to him, they changed their minds and said he was a god. There was an estate nearby that belonged to Publius, the chief official of the island. He welcomed us to his home and for three days entertained us hospitably. His father was sick in bed, suffering from fever and dysentery. Paul went in to see him and, after prayer, placed his hands on him and healed him. When this had happened, the rest of the sick on the island came and were cured. They honoured us in many ways and when we were ready to sail, they furnished us with the supplies we needed. After three months we put out to sea in a ship that had wintered in the island. It was an Alexandrian ship with the figurehead of the twin gods Castor and Pollux. We put in at Syracuse and stayed there three days. From there we set sail and arrived at Rhegium. The next day the south wind came up, and on the following day we reached Puteoli.

Having got over her surprise at the seeming coincidence, Verity realised that anyone who knew their way around the New Testament would have turned to that passage while visiting Syracuse. Nevertheless, she experienced a strange sensation of tingling throughout her body, as she had when she had held the letter from Rabbi Gamaliel.

CHAPTER 5

The Letters

Saturday

The next morning, Crispin went for a run around the archaeological site and up a hill overlooking the city and the port. Via G.R. Rizzo was lined with grand villas, gated and guarded. Out of interest, he glanced at some of the names on the bell pushes. Two-thirds of the way along he felt a wave of fear as he read, 'Cesare Romano'. He hoped he hadn't been seen as he didn't want to draw attention to himself or engage Cesare's interest prematurely. Returning from breakfasting alone at the hotel's excellent buffet, he reflected that he could get used to this lifestyle. He extracted the letters from his room safe. The formerly brittle papyri had relaxed enough for him to unroll them. Starting with one from Gamaliel and weighing down just one section at a time, so that it could easily be re-rolled, Crispin got a block of paper from reception and began the time-consuming business of transcription. For the highly skilled, it would be obvious where the words divided. Crispin's Greek was a bit rusty; he imagined Verity was having similar trouble.

*From Rabbi Gamaliel in Jerusalem to Marcus Antonius
Paulus (also known as Saul) in Caesarea. Greetings.*

I trust you are well and have not been the subject of any more unpleasantness. I have been deeply troubled by what you expressed to me on your last visit and have been wrestling with it ever since. Could that man, Jesus from Nazareth, really be our longed-for Messiah? I am aware he fulfils many of our scriptural prophesies, although some are so opaque it might be hard to recognise them in the flesh. Jesus was certainly not what we had all imagined and hoped for in a Messiah. I have attempted to be systematic and re-read the scriptures bearing him in mind. Nazareth was a puzzle; can anything good come out of there? Then I learned from Peter and John, whom I have visited several times at night, that Jesus was born in Bethlehem, as foretold by our prophet Micah:

And thou Bethlehem, in the land of Judah, art not the least among the princes of Judah: for out of thee shall come a Governor, that shall rule my people Israel.

They also have a genealogy constructed by Matthew, the former tax collector, whom Jesus attracted as a follower, which indicates he is a direct descendant of King David or at least his father, Joseph, was. His mother Mary may well have been related to Joseph. However, I am not convinced, as I have heard that there is another ancestor list which takes an entirely different route between David's son King Solomon and Joseph.

The stories surrounding Jesus' birth do seem very unusual. Shepherds coming into town having abandoned their flocks, claiming to have seen angels with a message for his mother, finding a baby in a stable, and worshipping him as if he were G_d! Not that I've ever had much to do with shepherds but they don't seem prone to hallucinations. As for those rich, exotic visitors from the East, Stargazers, highly educated men, claiming to have followed a moving heavenly body all the way from Persia to little Bethlehem? No wonder King Herod was alarmed. And their gifts: gold, frankincense and myrrh: kingship, divinity and death. Are these modern-day prophecies? I struggle to think so.

I realise now that I met this Jesus when he was a boy. He was the one who got left behind by his parents in Jerusalem just after Passover, and hung around the Temple engaging anyone he could find with his questions. He asked me about the identity of Abraham's three visitors by the oaks of Mamre. The ones who told Abraham and Sarah that they would have a son, even though both of them were very old. Scripture says that the 'Lord' appeared to Abraham. There were three of them but they always spoke in unison. Abraham addressed them as if they were one, as 'Lord,' and offered them hospitality. When they told him and Sarah that they would have a son, she, out of sight, laughed silently in disbelief, but they knew she had laughed and commented upon it. That boy Jesus asked me, 'Who is this three-in-one Lord?' I muttered something about it being a mystery; in fact I made my excuses and left.

The priests and rabbis talked about him for some time afterwards, as he seemed most unusual and had remarkable insights. Rabbi Caiaphas had a run-in with him, something to do with the hypocrisy of what priests preach versus how they live. Seemingly it was not the last time.

Throughout our history we, G_d's chosen people, have had men and women raised up and anointed by G_d as prophets. Some also had the gift of healing, and even of raising people from the dead, as did Elijah and Elisha. They tended to be very unpopular with our ruling authorities as they declared G_d's displeasure at our disobedience and idolatry. Many died at the hands of those authorities. I can see how Jesus might fit into this line. I have heard stories where, on being touched by him, the blind regained their sight, the lame walked, lepers were cleansed, the deaf had their hearing restored and that even one or two dead people were resuscitated. I simply don't know how much of this to believe. I am aware that Jesus preached that the kingdom of heaven was at hand and that those who heard him should repent and hear that good news. If true, these things certainly made your Jesus a prophet anointed by G_d, but do not necessarily make him the Messiah that we are awaiting. Especially as he is now dead.

I do remember when the one they called John the Baptiser was baptising people in the River Jordan and urging them to repent of their sins. I had travelled up north to see what he was doing and I listened to him. While I was there, a man who also seemed to have some followers came and asked John to baptise him. John seemed astonished and wished to defer to this man but he said no, to fulfil all righteousness John should baptise him. As he came out of the water there seemed to be a rumble of thunder and a strange light swirled over his head. I asked John about that incident and his words have never left me, 'This is Jesus, the lamb of G_d, who has come to save Israel from its sins.'

When did G_d send a lamb to save Israel? Obviously, on the night of the Israelite's exodus from Egypt, when we were to escape our physical slavery, G_d ordered us to slaughter a lamb and place its blood on the lintels and doorposts of our houses. That night he sent his Angel of Death and killed all the first-born sons of Egypt, except those who were saved by the blood of the lamb. Is that what John was alluding to? I wonder if even he knew?

You have left me much to think and pray about. May G_d go with you in all your endeavours. May he bless you, and keep you, may he make his face shine upon you and give you peace, now and always.

Your good friend and teacher
Gamaliel

★★★

Verity relished the task ahead of her. It felt like being a student again, wrestling with classical texts where interpreting what is meant cannot always be immediately discerned from the words written. This phenomenon is most commonly found in legal documents. She reckoned that modern English ones produced much the same challenges, which, she suspected, were written using opaque terms to keep the legal profession a closed shop, their output inaccessible to the untrained.

Verity had also picked up paper from reception and now delicately opened a letter from Gamaliel. She and Crispin had split those between them, agreeing to tackle them first. Separating out the words took all her concentration. Initially she skipped some that seemed ambiguous, planning to return to them later. She thought that once a translation started to emerge they'd become clearer.

Two hours passed before she got up to stretch and have a coffee. She wondered how Crispin was getting on, but didn't want to disturb him. They had agreed to meet up for lunch to discuss progress. She went up to the roof terrace by the pool and ordered an espresso, just managing to resist the offer of a pastry to go with it. Looking out over the skyline she recalled her time in Michigan where she had learned how to handle papyrus scrolls. She smiled to herself as she remembered Guidoriccio Fogliano. He was an American of Italian extraction who was sponsored by the New York office of Sotheby's auction house. On the same training course, they had hit it off instantly and enjoyed a delightful romance throughout that summer. Guidoriccio was not especially tall, but dark and handsome with wavy hair and the most impossibly long eyelashes framing come-to-bed eyes. His paternal grandparents were first-generation Americans, having emigrated between the world wars. They had run a trattoria in New York's Little Italy but were determined that their children should take as much advantage of their New World opportunities as possible. All four sons worked their way through college. Guidoriccio's father became an art historian and finally a curator at New York's Metropolitan Museum of Art.

Apart from his eyes, Verity was struck by his name, and had asked him if he was related to the famous thirteenth-century nobleman Guidoriccio da Fogliano. He'd laughed, delighted that someone should recognise it. She remembered him saying, 'I guess my family would sure like to think so. They did originate from near Fogliano but I suspect they may have adopted a more classy name when they landed at Ellis Island. When I visited Siena last fall, I made a point of going to see his fresco by Simone Martini on the wall of the Palazzo Publico.'

He had pulled out his phone, swiped though some pictures and showed Verity one he had taken with the 'No Photographs' sign prominently in front of it. He and she had gelled at that moment.

Their parting was more sorrowful than sweet. They had promised to keep in touch, agreeing that London to New York was an easy flight, but life and work had taken over. Guidoriccio was establishing himself as medieval and ancient manuscript expert at Sotheby's and Verity had also built her career. She wondered what had happened to him. Not for the first time she felt lonely and somewhat empty. I would like to share my life with someone, she thought. I'm not bothered about having children, but I don't want to remain alone. A wave of self-pity momentarily engulfed her. Pulling herself together, she was about to return to her room when Crispin appeared, also needing a break.

'I've got one or two gaps where I can't quite make out the writing and wondered if you could help me,' he said.

'So have I, and I'd appreciate some of your biblical knowledge. Catholic instruction, at any rate for children, is less than rigorous. Shall we try and work on them together, or at least in the same room?'

Crispin readily agreed to this, and Verity led the way down.

From Rabbi Gamaliel in Jerusalem to Marcus Antonius Paulus (also known as Saul) in Caesarea. Greetings

This is my second letter to you as I continue to wrestle with your extraordinary claims regarding the crucified Jesus. You have pointed me to those passages in the prophet Isaiah which talk of the suffering servant, but we have always regarded Israel as that servant. I concede that there are parallels with Isaiah's description and the scripture, but could that not be just coincidence? We Jews specialise in suffering. Are you saying that this Jesus represents the whole of Israel? How is that possible? All the same, I quote some Isaiah passages that would tie in with Jesus' life and the manner of his death.

Behold my servant, whom I uphold; mine elect, in whom my soul delighteth; I have put my spirit upon him: he shall bring forth judgment to the Gentiles. He shall not cry, nor cause his voice to be heard in the street. A bruised reed shall he not break, ... he shall bring forth judgment unto truth.... Thus saith G_d, he that created the heavens, ... he that spread forth the earth, ...; he that giveth breath unto the people upon it, and spirit to them that walk therein: I the Lord have called thee in righteousness, and will hold thine hand, and will keep thee, and give thee for a covenant of the people, for a light of the Gentiles; To open the blind eyes, to bring out the prisoners from the prison, and them that sit in darkness out of the prison house.

This Jesus must have been anointed by G_d to have been able to heal the sick and release those whose minds were imprisoned. He consorted with Samaritans, Romans, bleeding women and other unclean persons. He did these things in an un-showy way, unlike various false, charlatan prophets. Are the eyes of my heart spiritually blind?

He is despised and rejected of men; a man of sorrows, ... he was despised and we esteemed him not.

That part is true of Jesus, but also of Israel, when considered by the rest of the world.

Surely he hath borne our griefs, and carried our sorrows: yet we did esteem him stricken, smitten of G_d, and afflicted. But he was wounded for our transgressions, he was bruised for our iniquities ... and with his stripes we are healed.

How can we know that these prophecies refer to Jesus? He was savagely flogged but now he is dead.

All we like sheep have gone astray; we have turned every one to his own way; and the Lord hath laid on him the iniquity of us all. He was oppressed ... yet he opened not his mouth: he is brought as a lamb to the slaughter. ... He was taken from prison and from judgment: ... for the transgression of my people was he stricken. And he made his grave with the wicked, and with the rich in his death; because he had done no violence, neither was any deceit in his mouth.

The Sanhedrin certainly put on a mock trial, Jesus got no justice there. When questioned by Procurator Pontius Pilate, Jesus was silent, refusing to counter the accusations made against him. He was crucified with two notorious villains, and

Joseph of Arimathea, one of our wealthiest citizens, placed him in his own family tomb. All that correlates. However, I still struggle with the corollary of the next part of Isaiah, except that I know that the timing of the Lord is not our timing. You are convinced that Jesus was resurrected on the third day, and will return again in triumph and clouds of glory to judge the living and the dead and whose kingdom will have no end.

Therefore will I divide him a portion with the great ... because he hath poured out his soul unto death ... and he bare the sin of many, and made intercession for the transgressors.

If all this is true, we who reject Jesus as our G_d-sent saviour should be very afraid.

★ ★ ★

'How many prophecies are there in the Old Testament that could relate to Jesus?' asked Verity.

'It rather depends. Some claim hundreds. The Hebrew Scriptures, what we call the Old Testament, are a series of books of different genres, history, poetry and prophecy, among others. Theologians looking for prophecies concerning Jesus, and so with a Christian perspective, have found many parallels. To my mind some are more convincing than others, as you can always discern patterns in a large dataset if you want them badly enough.'

Verity smiled, 'Wishful thinking distorting the truth?'

'What is truth? as Pilate asked Jesus,' said Crispin. 'I put a break in the transcript here, as the next section seems to have been written later, you can see that there's a change in ink colour.'

I remember that extraordinary Passover. Before light we were disturbed by a noisy group of men hustling down the street past our family's house. Later our doorman told us that it was a troop of the Temple guards who had arrested a man and were taking him to the High Priest's house. A most irregular time for such an action. After a while, a larger group tramped back towards the Antonia fortress, residence of the Procurator. There was quite a commotion coming from that direction, so I decided to go and see what was happening, much to my wife's annoyance, as this was going to be a busy day without additional distractions.

Procurator Pontius Pilate had come out onto the steps, in order that the priests did not have to enter a Gentile building on Passover preparation day, thus avoiding the need to re-purify themselves. They accused Jesus of Nazareth of blasphemy, as he had been declared to be the Son of G_d by his disciples and he would not deny that acclamation. The priests demanded that he be put to death. Quite a rabble had assembled.

Pilate asked for evidence that Jesus had broken any Roman law. He wasn't too bothered about the intricacies of Jewish laws. He left those to the Temple. I heard various witnesses being called, but they seemed to contradict each other. The High Priest, Caiaphas, claimed that Jesus was a threat to public order as he had declared himself to be the King of the Jews, in direct opposition to his Imperial Majesty, Emperor Tiberius. Jesus refused to answer Pilate's questions and, when challenged with his claim to be King of the Jews, stated that his kingdom was not of this world and that Pilate only had authority over him because it had been granted to him from above. Pilate became exasperated and was going to release Jesus but the priests managed to whip up the crowd into a state of hysteria, baying, 'Crucify him! Crucify him!' The situation was degenerating fast and I considered it prudent to leave, as the behaviour of hot-blooded crowds can be very unpredictable.

Apparently there were already two men due to be crucified on that day, which was surprising, as no one ever wanted the process to extend into the Sabbath, especially a Great Sabbath, such as this one, with Passover falling on Saturday. As you know, it can take several days for crucified men to die.

Crispin paused and looked up at Verity, whose eyes were wide with wonder.

She said, 'This is a non-Christian source seeming to confirm some of the finer details in the Gospels recounted by a Jewish onlooker. The Vatican will be thrilled, and those who deny the historicity of Jesus and the stories surrounding him will have a problem on their hands.'

'Oh they can always declare that this is a fake, as they do with other ancient texts,' said Crispin. 'I've even encountered a Classist in Cambridge who declared that the stone inscription found in Caesarea Philippi that mentions Pontius Pilate was made up.' He returned to his translation.

Around mid-day I went up to the Temple with our servant, Jacob, to purchase and offer a lamb to be slaughtered by the priest for our evening Passover feast. I thought we'd be in plenty of time, but I should have gone earlier, just as my wife had told me to do.

The waiting crowd had spilled out of the Temple courtyard and well down the street, with men jostling each other, already frustrated by the delay. There was a troop of Roman guards stationed outside to keep order. They looked anxious and I heard the centurion ask for reinforcements. When we finally got through the gateway, the Temple guards were straining to keep order. It was heaving. The sacrificial lambs were corralled in a corner of the courtyard. They struggled, panicking, bleating piteously and climbing on each other to try to escape. The smell of fear and blood coupled with death cries filled the air. When men went to select the next one, lambs fell over each other in terror. Their excrement was everywhere. So much for purity.

The Temple had five slaughtering stations; the High Priest presided over the central one and officials singled out Jerusalem's more prominent citizens to have their lamb sacrificed by him.

A storm was brewing and the sky became darker and darker. It felt eerie. Finally our turn came and, having been given a decent looking specimen, I was ushered up to the High Priest's table. All this had taken some three hours. By then the sky was almost black and the air seemed to crackle. At the moment my lamb's throat was slit there was an almighty flash and an explosion of thunder. Lightning forked down, hit the Temple's Holy of Holies and shards of blinding fire skittered across the paving. An earthquake knocked us to the ground. Blocks of stone fell from the parapets, shattering. Chaos. Shouting and screaming. The lambs escaped from their pen and careered round. I was getting to my feet and checking on Jacob, when one of the High Priest's servants ran from the inner sanctum and blurted out that the veil screening the Holy of Holies, where the Ark of the Covenant used to rest, and where the presence of G_d was deemed to dwell, had been ripped in two!

A catastrophe had occurred, but none of us knew what it meant.

Both Verity and Crispin found themselves experiencing strange sensations, even though Crispin had read this account earlier. The skin on the back of their skulls seemed to tighten, a nervy tingling filled their bodies and a high-pitched sound, like tinnitus, afflicted them both. As the sensations faded, Crispin took a deep breath and continued.

Eventually Jacob and I got home. The women were frantic, as

the lamb should have been prepared for roasting ages earlier. Getting a charcoal oven to stay at the right temperature for an extended time period was no trivial matter, as I was repeatedly told. I was in deep trouble but not minded to explain. I sensed something significant had occurred, though I'd no idea what. I left poor Jacob to take the heat from the kitchen.

During the following week, strange rumours circulated in Jerusalem, claiming that this Jesus had been raised from the dead. The tomb was undoubtedly empty, despite guards having been posted. I dismissed this as outlandish speculation and assumed that his disciples had spirited his body away and were now claiming his resurrection in order to fulfil prophecies concerning our expected Messiah. It seemed to be the only rational explanation. However, doubts did enter my mind over the following months as increasing numbers of people claimed to have seen and touched the risen Jesus. To my mind more significantly, Jesus' followers continued to insist, to the point of their own deaths, that he was still alive, that Jesus was our expected Messiah and that he had come to save us from our sins by being sacrificed and making atonement to G_d in our stead. Had these disciples known those claims to be lies, maintaining them through torture to death was to me inconceivable.

I recall you telling me about a certain Stephen whom you saw stoned to death for just such blasphemous pronouncements. It seems you have been wholly converted to his point of view.

I shall consider further all these matters. If what you claim is true, this is the most significant G_d-given event since the Exodus. If not, I fear my most promising pupil is not only deluded but is also in danger of an early death.

May you be blessed in every way and may the Lord keep you safe and in your right mind.

Gamaliel

'This is extraordinary!' Verity exclaimed. 'This must be the only eye witness account of Jesus' trial and death apart from the Gospels. A contemporaneous record, even if from the Temple's location, which makes it all the more realistic for me. Is there anything else like this, apart from that passing comment in Josephus' apologetic written for the Romans, the *Antiquities of the Jews*?'

'Not that I know of, and many scholars think Josephus' account has been tampered with, as it sounds rather too Christian to be written by an unconverted Jew. Tacitus also refers to Jesus' existence in passing. This account seems to confirm the Gospel versions in all their details. The Church should be thrilled.'

'So far so good but we might find some more controversial material that they would be tempted to suppress.'

Crispin grinned at her. He did like Verity. She had an open mind but a clear eye for political intrigue and subterfuge. Thinking of subterfuge, he wondered again how they were going to get the scrolls back into the chest undetected.

From Rabbi Gamaliel in Jerusalem to Marcus Antonius
Paulus (also known as Saul) in Caesarea. Greetings

I have now had an opportunity to read the draft of the letter which you are planning to send to Rome. I always knew you were my cleverest student, but here your reasoning has challenged both my comprehension and my beliefs.

I agree with you that the original order of the world that which G_d created and found to be very good was thrown out of joint when Adam sinned by eating the one thing that had been forbidden him: the fruit from the tree of the knowledge of good and evil. He and Eve certainly gained that knowledge, but it didn't do them any good, falling from grace, cast out of paradise and having to toil all the days of their life, with the added grief of one of their sons murdering the other. In having freedom of choice, and choosing disobedience, they allowed sin to enter the world and infect the whole of creation. I agree with your view that this was not G_d's original plan and he wished to find a means to restore creation to its pre-fallen state.

G_d chose Abraham to be the father of nations and through his descendants to bring about restitution. Then we get to Moses who, having led the Israelites out of slavery in Egypt, was given the Law on Mount Sinai. The Law was to help us live without sin, and again, I have to concede your point that it managed to achieve quite the opposite effect. Our wilfulness and blindness to G_d's holy law, the attraction of selfish behaviour, even when we don't want to live that way, seems to overwhelm us.

I have re-studied the ten commandments in the light of your letter.

I am the Lord thy G_d, who hath brought thee out of the land of Egypt, out of the house of bondage. Thou shalt have no other gods before me.

Thou shalt not make any graven image, or any likeness of anything that is in heaven above, or that is in the earth beneath, or that is in the water under the earth. Thou shalt not bow down thyself to them, nor serve them, for I the Lord thy G_d am a jealous G_d, visiting the iniquity of the fathers upon the children unto the third and fourth generation of them that hate me, and showing mercy unto thousands of them that love me, and keep my commandments.

This is one of the difficulties we Jews have with our Roman masters, refusing to worship the Emperor as a god. But it is not as simple as that. Repeatedly we have been beguiled into honouring or even worshiping the gods of the Canaanites and the other tribes around us, especially when we have married into their families. We may think that setting up a sacred pole on a high place is harmless, but we have deceived ourselves. Even more pernicious are the gods we set up in our hearts and in our homes. Our worship and love of money, of power, possessions, material and mental comfort, social position, family advancement, of being seen to consort with the right people. Which of us is innocent of these?

Thou shalt not take the name of the Lord thy G_d in vain; for the Lord will not hold him guiltless that taketh his name in vain.

Which of us has made a vow in G_d's name and not broken it?

Remember the sabbath day, to keep it holy. Six days shalt thou labour, and do all thy work, but the seventh day is the sabbath of the Lord thy G_d. In it thou shalt not do any work, thou, nor thy son, nor thy daughter, thy manservant, nor thy maidservant, nor thy cattle, nor the stranger that is within thy gates. For in six days the Lord made heaven and earth, the sea, and all that in them is, and rested the seventh day, wherefore the Lord blessed the sabbath day, and hallowed it.

Outwardly we are perhaps even over-careful regarding sabbath observance, to the extent that acts of mercy may be eschewed in case they may be construed as 'work'. But again, in our minds, have we worried about business issues, planned ventures, or managed our accounts, when we should have been resting in the love of G_d?

Honour thy father and thy mother: that thy days may be long upon the land which the Lord thy G-d giveth thee.

It is of course our duty, but goodness, can't mothers and fathers be maddening!

Thou shalt not kill.

Except where the Lord has sanctioned a holy war. Yet our anger at times may boil over into the desire to kill, even if we avoid the act. We even kill the things we love by striking a vicious blow, casting a bitter look or speaking a flattering word. I heard that this Jesus even preached that we should love our enemies! Unrealistic wouldn't you say?

Thou shalt not commit adultery.

That of course is abusing another man's possession, whether his daughter or his wife. Our wives seem to get very upset about it. And as for women straying, who wants to find they have unknowingly brought up another man's child? That plays merry hell with family inheritance. However, it is hard not to look at all those pretty girls and just dream.

Thou shalt not steal.

It goes without saying. Though, have I always been scrupulous about pointing out a merchant's error in my favour? Or have I rationalised it that such errors probably balance out in the end? Is avoiding paying taxes to our Roman overlords a patriotic act or stealing in the eyes of G_d?

Crispin interjected, 'Jesus was challenged on whether Jews should pay Roman taxes, to try and trick him into condoning tax evasion. D'you remember? He asked whose head was stamped on the coin and when they admitted it was Caesar's, Jesus said "render unto Caesar that which is Caesar's and to God that which is God's".

When are the spoils of war stealing? Should we let people become so destitute that they are reduced to stealing and then blame only them? Is deliberately running up debts knowing they will be redeemed in the year of Jubilee stealing?

Thou shalt not bear false witness against thy neighbour.

Law courts, obviously, but gossip? When does that become slander? Innuendo, destroying a man's reputation with no possibility of redress in order to damage his position?

Thou shalt not covet thy neighbour's house. Thou shalt not covet thy neighbour's wife, nor his manservant, nor his maidservant, nor his ox, nor his ass, nor any thing that is thy neighbour's.

Envy, jealousy, covetousness. They sour relationships, create dissatisfaction, create a false sense of entitlement, make you feel resentful and bitter. They damage the soul. These sins are hard to avoid when you see the successful flaunting their wealth and claiming that their prosperity demonstrates that they are blessed by G_d for their righteous living.

I am not surprised over the years that our priests have created hundreds of extra laws to try to fill in the gaps since, when you study these ten, they are not a simple as they first appear.

My dear Saul, you are so right that the Law seems to

highlight our sinful behaviour rather than preventing it. Why do we do that which we don't want to do and yet fail to do those things which we do want to do? How wretched is all humanity in general and Israel in particular, we who have had G_d to guide us for so long! We Jews, who should be the light of the world, have led it into darkness. As you say, the wages of sin are death. We have allowed the world to sink into futility and corruption, when we should have been offering it salvation though our relationship with the Lord. I despair as I think of it. Whatever is to be done?

Your claim of what G_d has in fact done to rescue us from the situation from Adam onwards is, however, so awesome that I must ponder and pray about it further before I can begin to organise my thoughts. If what you say is true, this Jesus has completely turned worshipping in the Temple on its head and much of our own way of life with it. Such views are highly dangerous and could be the death of you. You do know that, don't you?

May G_d go with you in all you do and preserve you in safety.

Gamaliel

'Crispin, don't you think it odd that God would fall prey to the law of unintended consequences? Couldn't he tell in advance that, given free will and the sight of something that looked tempting and sounded exciting, we would fall for it, if not every time, then frequently? Isn't God supposed to be omniscient? First we have the probably metaphorical fall of Adam and Eve and then the complete failure of Israel to live by the Ten Commandments.'

'Paul's theory was that God did know in advance but he allowed this failure to happen so he could come to earth in the person of Jesus to take all the consequences of our sin, thereby confirming God's righteousness and justice. Sin is not a consequence-free phenomenon, but must be punished prior to reconciliation. However, he took the punishment upon himself. Paul's belief was that this gave God the opportunity to gather in the Gentile world and he saw his own mission as doing just that.'

Verity thought for a bit. 'It seems a very convoluted way of going about things but I suppose if we didn't have the free will to go off the rails we would be puppets or automata.'

'Shall we look at one of Mama's letters for a bit of light relief? I've got into her handwriting now and my Aramaic is coming along leaps and bounds.'

> From Bernice, widow of Marcus Antonius Lucius residing in Tarsus, to Marcus Antonius Paulus in Corinth, Greetings.

> My darling Sauli
> It is so long since I have heard from you and you know how I worry. You seem to write to all sorts of people, but you never write to me, your poor old Mama.

> I have heard such terrible reports of the dreadful things people are saying about you and that you have been beaten by the synagogue! You will be careful won't you? I have found a nice girl for you who would make you a lovely wife, but you must hurry home for her. Otherwise her father will marry her off to Benjamin, the rabbi's second son, and have you had your eyebrows seen to? I know you can't help going bald so young, it runs in the family, but them meeting in the middle is unfortunate and you must appear at your best on your return to secure a wife.

> You'll never guess, Rachel, the eldest daughter of Ruben Levy, you know the one who is so proud of his moral uprightness and how strictly his wife Naomi has brought up the family, well Rachel has only gone and got herself pregnant

by a Roman soldier! Of course she has been disowned by her family and neighbours. The garrison is being sent home on leave soon to a place called Britannia, wherever that is. I gather it rains a lot. Rachel is going with them. Naomi has left our sewing circle in shame. I know it's not really funny but you should see that stuck-up family now!

Your brother-in-law Eli is doing really well keeping our family tent-making business thriving, though I am sure he would benefit from your help. But you were always such a clever boy and so studious. I have to believe that Abba did the right thing sending you to study theology with Rabbi Gamaliel in Jerusalem but I do miss you so. Your younger sister Livia has grown into a beautiful young woman and we are looking out for a husband for her. Do try not to get yourself into any more trouble. The synagogue is one thing but the Romans are not to be trifled with, citizen or no citizen.

I hear strange reports that you think that people of that breakaway sect, the Way or whatever they call themselves, are correct and that the Messiah has come and gone. For someone so clever, sometimes you are such a silly boy, of course he hasn't, or he would have driven the Romans out of Judea. I don't know where you get your ideas from. Anyhow, all these things are far too complicated for me. All I know is that following the death of dear Abba, you should be here as head of our household and not gadding about entertaining weird religious ideas, and expecting me to take all the domestic decisions and keep the servants in order. It is such a strain on my nerves. I do so worry about you. I must stop now as the ship carrying this is about to depart. Please write soon.

Your worrying and loving Mama, Bernice

'I'll bet Paul had very mixed feeling when reading that letter,' commented Verity. 'On the one hand he had escaped a stifling domestic domain and probably a parochially minded society. On the other hand, compared with the life of a wandering preacher transmitting a highly controversial message, domestic security must have seemed attractive at times.'

'Shall I read her next one?'

Verity nodded.

From Bernice, widow of Marcus Antonius Lucius residing in Tarsus, to Marcus Antonius Paulus, Greetings.

My darling Sauli

I do hear such distressing accounts of you. My poor nerves. Do you have no sympathy for your wretched mother all those miles away? And you hardly ever write. I just pick up bits and pieces from returning travellers. Do you know how embarrassing that is? What has happened to you? You used to be so dutiful, but now you seem nothing like the lovely boy I struggled to bring up. You were always wilful but now you are being so heartless to you poor old mama. I do suffer so.

I cannot believe that you have been beaten with rods! You, a Roman citizen! That is illegal and they know it, or didn't you tell them in time? Surely you are carrying your bronze citizenship plaque with you? You haven't lost it, have you? Otherwise you'll have to get a copy from Rome and think how long that will take, not to mention the expense.

Your grandfather was so proud to be granted citizenship by Imperator Marcus Antonius. Of course he did supply his army with a huge number of tents at a very good price, but even so, you cannot take these things for granted. Lucky his citizenship came through before the battle of Actium, or it might never have happened.

'Gosh,' said Verity, 'that makes so much sense. Paul came from Tarsus, in what's now Turkey, and that's where Mark Antony had his fleet stationed in order to invade Parthia in 41BC. What troops need are tents. It seems Paul's grandfather supplied them and was awarded Roman citizenship. It was customary to take the name of your sponsor as part of your Roman name, hence all these letters addressed to Marcus Antonius Paulus. I'd wondered about that.

That makes total sense of the inscription on the plaque:

Crispin's eyes lit up, 'Isn't it that occasion in Shakespeare's *Antony and Cleopatra* when Cleopatra turns up, you remember,

The barge she sat in, like a burnish'd throne, burned on the water: the poop was beaten gold; purple the sails, and so perfumed that the winds were lovesick with them; the oars were silver, which to the tune of flutes kept stroke, and made the water which they beat to follow faster, as amorous of their strokes.

'It makes it all come alive. Though on second thoughts it sounds a bit like *Bella Donna's* interior decor,' winced Verity.

Crispin continued reading.

You'll never guess! That old rogue Laban down the road has been caught selling his lame donkey to a man from the next town. We of course all knew she was lame, but somehow he managed to dose her up with willow bark, you know, that infusion I take for my headaches. Oh I am such a martyr to my headaches. Well Laban had dosed her up for a couple of days, taken her to market and sold her. Unfortunately for him, a neighbour told the buyer that the ass had always been lame and good for little, so he came into town demanding his money back, leading the poor, limping creature. There was such a row! The whole street came out to watch! Eventually, despite many protestations and swearing on the lives of his children, which seemed a bit risky to me, Laban gave in and handed the money back.

'No wonder Paul was keen to move on to Spain after Rome. Imagine going home to that!' exclaimed Crispin.

'He didn't seem keen to marry, did he?'

'He wrote that it was better to marry than to burn with passion,' continued Crispin. 'But Paul was driven by his passion for transmitting the Gospel as he saw it. He could hardly have dragged a wife and kids along with him. There is a later writing called Paul and Thecla, which may be complete fantasy. In it there is a physical description of Paul as being short, bald, with bandy legs and a mono-brow, which is how some fourth-century frescos have depicted him,'

'Hardly film-star stuff. Am I right in remembering that willow bark, which Bernice mentions, was used by the Romans as a painkiller and is the origin of aspirin?'

'Yes, and the ancient Egyptians had developed opium from poppy seeds. They've found traces of it in ointment jars shaped like upturned poppy heads. Not much is new.'

'Is there anything you don't know, Crispin?'

He laughed. 'I'm just an inveterate snapper-up of unconsidered trifles.'

From Rabbi Gamaliel in Jerusalem to Marcus Antonius Paulus (also known as Saul) in Caesarea.

Greetings, I am so astonished by the next part of your draft letter to Rome, that I have copied it here, as if by writing it out myself, I can begin to understand it better, if at all.

There is therefore now no condemnation for those who are in Christ Jesus. For the law of the Spirit of life in Christ Jesus has set you free from the law of sin and of death. For G_d has done what the law, weakened by the flesh, could not do, by sending his own Son in the likeness of sinful flesh, and to deal with sin, he condemned sin in the flesh, so that the just requirement of the law might be fulfilled in us, who walk not according to the flesh but according to the Spirit. For those who live according to the flesh set their minds on the things of the flesh, but those who live according to the Spirit set their minds on the things of the Spirit. To set the mind on the flesh is death, but to set the mind on the Spirit is life and peace. For this reason the mind that is set on the flesh is hostile to G_d; it does not submit to G_d's law — indeed it cannot, and those who are in the flesh cannot please G_d.

I know you are writing to those who believe, as you do, that Jesus is the Messiah, the Christ, which makes sense of the next passage, but this is more than revolutionary. If true, G_d has stepped into the world at this very moment to restore us back to a pre-fallen state. It does not appear to have been an obvious success so far, but I shall persevere in studying your reasoning.

By 'flesh' I take it you mean not just our physical selves, but all of us and other creatures who share the corruptibility and mortality of the world; the disintegration and decay of physical creation. By 'Spirit' here I am assuming you mean primarily the Spirit of G_d, the Holy Spirit.

But you are not in the flesh; you are in the Spirit, since the Spirit of G_d dwells in you. Anyone who does not have the Spirit of Christ does not belong to him. But if Christ is in you, though the body is dead because of sin, the Spirit is life because of righteousness. If the Spirit of him who raised Jesus from the dead dwells in you, he who raised Christ from the dead will give life to your mortal bodies also through his Spirit that dwells in you.

An implication of this, which you expand on later, is that non-Jews, pagan Gentiles, are on an equal footing with us in potentially having the Spirit of G_d dwelling in them. The promise was given through us but now you suggest it is equally open to everyone. A lot of Jews are going to be really upset by that idea. Of course some Gentiles were folded into our Jewish family; for example Ruth, who was a Moabite but became King David's great-grandmother. Our father Abraham was promised by G_d that he would be the father of many nations. I had assumed that they would all become Jewish, but maybe not? Salvation through faith, faith in Jesus you call the Christ, not bloodline? You refer to the prophet Hosea, who spoke the word of G-d saying:

Those who were not my people I will call 'my people, and her who was not beloved I will call 'beloved'. And in the very place where it was said to them, 'You are not my people' there they shall be called 'children of the living God'.

The difficulty I have is that this could refer to Gentiles now but also perhaps to others at some other time. It is very hard to tell.

To finish, I come to your reiteration of Leviticus 19:18 'You shall love your neighbour as yourself.' Who is my neighbour? Is he or she now, as you suggest both Jew and Gentile, male and female, slave and free? Is this the message Jesus came to bring? Could he really be our Messiah? I am baffled. However I am encouraged by your statement that, 'We know that all things work together for good for those who love G_d, who are called according to his purpose.'

Your proviso in the next line gives me pause for thought. *'For those whom he foreknew he also predestined to be conformed to the image of his Son, in order that he might be the firstborn within a large family. And those whom he predestined he also called; and those whom he called he also justified; and those whom he justified he also glorified.'*

My dear Saul, you have given me so much to think and pray about. Please do keep in touch, and perhaps you could bring yourself to write to your mother once in a while. I know she does so long to hear from you.

This comes with my prayers and blessing.

Gamaliel

'Is what he's quoting from Paul's letter to the Romans?' asked Verity.

'Yes, and here we have excerpts from it that are way before our earliest extant copy.'

'Oh that's P46 isn't it? I saw part of it in Michigan University when I was on summer school there studying the handling and renovation of papyri. I recall it's dated to around AD 200.

Crispin grinned at her.

'I think I'm lettered-out Crispin, fancy a drink?'

CHAPTER 6

Santa Maria delle Lacrime

Sunday

Having breakfasted late, Verity and Crispin walked to Santa Maria delle Lacrime in good time for mid-morning Mass. The circular structure had many entrances and they chose the nearest. Walking up a steep ramp they entered through a small tunnel into a vast open space, the roof being self-supporting from its perimeter. It was light, airy and exuded a sense of peaceful calm. The floor of polished marble had a design like that of a ship's compass in white, beige and greys radiating from under the dome's apex.

Immediately to their left was one of the series of chapels which flanked the perimeter. This held a full-sized replica of the Shroud of Turin, with a brief explanation and a photograph showing it in negative. From a distance, first they at found it hard to interpret what they were seeing, since the most visible marks were those of a burnt diamond pattern which was repeated several times along its length. This was the result of the folded shroud having been in a silver casket, which partially melted in a fire in 1532, burning through one corner. Allowing their eyes to adjust, gradually a faint brown image of two figures of a man head-to-head on the cream-coloured linen could be discerned. The one on the right was face up, the other face down. Both heads were in the centre with the bodies extending along the shroud. The figure was heavily bearded, with what looked like a broken nose and a damaged eye. Their gaze was drawn to his crossed arms coming together at folded hands, the thumbs invisible. The photographic negative was startling. Although the eyes were shut, the image seemed to be examining them.

They went and sat quietly a few rows from the front on one of the large semicircular movable wooden pews. Tourists and visitors milled around. Two young women, both wearing t-shirts and tight jeans, which showed off their generous curves, lit multiple candles on the pair of three-tiered circular metal stands. They then prepared the altar area, removing rope barriers. Gradually the seating filled with around two hundred people, who ranged from elderly, short, spherical ladies in black, through middle-aged locals to visitors. Verity and Crispin were the youngest by some margin. Crispin had picked up a couple of multi-lingual pamphlets giving the history of the church. He handed one to Verity and started to read the English translation:

In 1953 a newly married couple living in Syracuse were expecting their first baby. Their names were Angelo Iannuso and Antonina Lucia. It was a difficult pregnancy and Antonina suffered recurrent loss of her vision. At around three in the morning of the 29th August, her vision failed completely but, by eight-thirty, it had returned. Antonina then saw tears streaming down the face of the Madonna which was hanging at the head of her bed. The framed plaster effigy was a depiction of the Immaculate Heart of Maria and had been a wedding present.

The weeping repeated at various times between 29th August and the 1st September; news of which rapidly spread. The Ianusso's house became a place of incessant pilgrimage. It came to the notice of the Church. The local priest, Don Giuseppe Bruno, with the permission of the Vatican Curia, subjected the phenomenon to a scientific commission presided over by Dr Michele Cassola.

After examining the tears and the effigy, the commission concluded that the tears were human and that the phenomenon was not scientifically explicable. In December of that year the Bishop of Sicily declared the weeping authentic. The effigy, before it was housed in a sanctuary constructed for it, remained available for veneration by the faithful in Piazza Euripide.

Crispin looked up at the white marble altar wall, protestant in its simplicity. Set high within it was the plaster effigy. Light filtered through windowed slits running parallel to the roof's ribs. The building radiated calm. Crispin found himself surprisingly moved. He would love to be a father but didn't see how it could be possible. A stab of pain hit him. Why did his brother Hector have to die? Why couldn't he, Crispin, make his parents proud of him? Why did he have to be gay? He gazed at the effigy of the Madonna, his eyes clouded by tears. At least he had Hilary and he had God, he supposed.

Verity glanced at Crispin. She was highly sceptical of the supposedly weeping statue, but she realised that lots of people must have believed in it for this church to have been built in veneration. She concluded, with Hamlet, that perhaps there might be more things in heaven and earth than were dreamt of in her philosophy.

A cantor commenced singing into a microphone, generating a huge echo, eliding his words. Two priests emerged, one of whom had a moustache and pointy beard. Both Verity and Crispin were familiar with the order of service, as the English Reformation had retained the structure of the Latin Mass. Other protestant movements had dispensed with liturgy altogether. However, Crispin regretted the lack of hymns. Each of the young women read passages from the Bible and the junior priest read from John's Gospel. The once familiar words, even in translation, lulled Verity into a receptive reverie.

'Jesus said, "Do not let your hearts be troubled. Believe in God, believe also in me. In my Father's house there are many dwellings. If it were not so, would I have told you that I go to prepare a place for you? And if I go and prepare a place for you, I will come again and will take you to myself, so that where I am, there you may be also. And you know the way to the place where I am going." Thomas said to him, "Lord, we do not know where you are going. How can we know the way?" Jesus said to him, "*I am the way, and the truth, and the life. No one comes to the Father except through me.* If you know me, you will know my Father also. From now on you do know him and have seen him."'

The older priest took the microphone.

'Jesus said, "*I am the way and the truth and the life. No one comes to the Father except through me.*" What did Jesus mean by that? Did he mean that, as St Paul says, "If we declare that Jesus is Lord with our lips, and believe in our hearts that God raised him from the dead, we will be saved?" Yes, I believe he did mean that, but not in a narrow way. We must consider who Jesus really is. When he walked upon this earth, 2,000 years ago, he was the Word of God come in a physical form, fulfilling prophecies of the expected Jewish Messiah. He performed miracles and preached the coming of the Kingdom of God. This was so that those who encountered him had the opportunity to recognise and respond to him as he fulfilled prophesies that had been written about him in the Old Testament hundreds of years earlier. Not all did.

'St John's Gospel starts, "In the beginning was the Word, and the Word was with God and the Word was God ... everything that was made, was made by him." This is an echo of the opening lines of Genesis, the first book of the Bible, "In the beginning God created the heaven and the earth. And the earth was without form, and void; and darkness was upon the face of the deep. And the Spirit of God moved upon the face of the waters. And God said, Let there be light: and there was light."

'God spoke light and all of creation into being. His voice, the Word of God, effected creation while his Spirit hovered. The Trinity in action. Throughout the Old Testament, the Word of God spoke through his prophets as his Spirit infused them. Occasionally, even God the Father appears, generally in disguise, for example as a pillar of fire or smoke to guide the Israelites though forty years wandering in the wilderness. Only his back was visible to Moses who was hidden in the cleft of a rock. To Elijah he revealed himself as a still, small voice after a storm.

'The Word of God finally came to us in the form of the man Jesus, the promised Messiah, the Christ, the one anointed to bring salvation to fallen mankind. Fully human and fully God. Begotten not made, being of one substance with the Father by whom all things were made. Those Old Testament prophets, starting with Abraham, are in one of God's dwelling places now because they obeyed the Word of God, they trusted him.

'Jesus said, "*I am the way and the truth and the life. No one comes to the Father except through me.*" Now that Jesus has come, and we have his testimony and that of his apostles, is it possible to be saved if we don't declare with our lips that Jesus is Lord and believe in our hearts that God raised him from the dead? Traditional church teaching says no. At the risk of you all writing to the Bishop to complain about my heresy, I would like to say I am not absolutely certain that it is as harsh as that. Saint Paul recognised those holy non-Jews who acted justly and mercifully and walked humbly, even if they did not fully know the Jewish God. Such people are with us today. They may never have heard of Jesus through no fault of their own, although we are commanded by the Lord to make sure everyone has. They may have found it impossible to believe due to their life's experiences, or they may be so part of their own culture and religion that they are unable to break away. And yet they lead a life of love, joy, peace, patience, generosity, selflessness, forgiveness and grace. They rejoice in the *truth*, they have followed the *way*. Are they to be denied the *life*? Are they to be condemned to an eternity outside God's love and dwelling?

'Perhaps – and I only say *perhaps* – they will have an opportunity to acknowledge Jesus as their Lord and believe that God the Father raised him from the dead, once they have left this mortal life. I cannot believe that a God who loves all that he has made and declared it to be very good would not offer each of us a final chance to come to him through a conversation with Jesus, made visible, the way, the truth and the life.

'So does that mean it doesn't matter whether or not we believe in Jesus as the Word of God, but just lead a good life and hope for the best? *By no means!* For a start, we may not have an opportunity to turn to him after our bodily death. That I cannot promise. Jesus said he came to offer us life in all its fullness. We can begin to experience that the moment we acknowledge him as our Lord. We are freed from fears and self-imposed constraints to become fully the people we have the potential to be. Faith offers us a secure identity as a beloved child of God. From that place we need have no fear. We never again have to live up to others' expectations of us, but can be *true* to God and *true* to ourselves. We will walk in the *way*. We will live fully in this *life* and, finally, we will dwell in the house of the Lord for ever. Amen.'

Verity sat transfixed. It was as if everything the priest said was directed at her. She felt a tingling through her body, a lightness of being, a heightened awareness. Almost without realising it she joined the line of those going up to take communion. The priest took a wafer from the silver flat-bottomed bowl, in the centre of which was a chalice, dipped it into the wine and placed it on her tongue. Time stood still. His grey lined face dissolved into the strong smiling features of a bearded thirty-year old, with a broken nose, long brown hair and hypnotic eyes, compelling her gaze.

He said, 'Verity, take, eat, this is my body; which was given for you; this is my blood, which was shed for you. I died for you, I live for you. I love you. Follow me.' The vision faded and the patient priest smiled and gently indicated that perhaps she should move on.

Crispin followed her. Technically, as an Anglican, he was not welcome to take communion in a Roman Catholic Church, but he didn't think Jesus would mind. The sermon had touched him too. He began to think that perhaps he could live his life more openly, not living up to his parents' expectation. Hilary had a point. He knew that really. In accepting that he could never be Hector or straight, he might be able to live his life in more of its fullness. He guessed it was a process, but maybe this was a start?

CHAPTER 7

Augusto

Sunday

Augusto looked around, beaming fondly. He enjoyed those times when he could act the *pater familias*. He sat at the head of the table, with his mother, Gloria, on his right-hand side. Next to her sat his son and daughter-in-law, then a gap where the grandchildren had been at the beginning of the meal. On Augusto's left sat his sister Olivia, his wife's brother, Raimondo, further child-sized gaps, Raimondo's wife, Augusto's daughter and son-in-law, and Augusto's wife, Rena, at the far end. They were in the garden of the local trattoria under a canopy of vines. The air was heavy with the rich scent of ripened figs and drowsy wasps were getting drunk on some of the fallen fruit. A dramatic lily display in the centre of the table added to the perfume. He patted his mother's hand fondly, as Raimondo rose to give a speech. Earlier Augusto had made the opening speech of welcome and of celebration. It had been short and to the point, but full of heart-felt appreciation of his mother. He now refilled his glass of iced limoncello, as he knew this one could take some time. With a flourish Raimondo embarked on a history of the family and Gloria's role within it. He had done his homework. Raimondo was local politician and had the fulsome, florid delivery beloved of such types. Augusto allowed his mind to drift. Late last night he had emailed his boss at the Commission for Sacred Archaeology informing him of the false wall and chest. He had skimmed over exactly how they had discovered the wall was false, and hoped the subsequent treasure would preclude too many questions. He doubted the email would be read before Monday, but he explained about Santa Cecilia, and that he would not be contactable until Tuesday. The village had neither wi-fi nor mobile signal and not much in the way of landlines. It was as if time had stopped here fifty years ago. Augusto's mind was spinning. Was the chest locked? Would there be a key? Forcing it open would be heavily frowned upon in archaeological circles. What might it contain? It could be the most magnificent find, but whether they would be allowed to keep it to raise their tourist profile he doubted. Anything of any significance tended to be whisked away to the Vatican Archives for study. The mills of God grind slowly, but not at quite the glacial speed of the Vatican's. If the Cardinal who was the head of the Vatican Archives became involved, not even the University of Naples would get a look in.

Raimondo was still delivering his grandiose speech. 'When Gloria welcomed me into her family, it was among the most wonderful days of my life. I was so sorry never to have known her husband. He must have been a fine man by all accounts.'

Augusto winced. Not by *all* accounts. And who the hell did Raimondo think he was? Not even Gloria's son-in-law. But there was no stopping him.

Two of the grandsons came careering up on their bikes, skidded to a halt, scattering gravel and then shot off again, laughing. Their four-year-old sister staggered up crying as her ice cream had splattered out of its cone. Chocolate smeared her face and had splodged down her party frock. Her mother took her off to clean her up and console her.

Augusto continued to fret about the chest. Could they open it? What would it contain? Who should see it and when? How should they handle any publicity? What would the legal implications and ownership issues be?

He suspected that he wouldn't be able to stop himself popping into the office on their return home on Monday to check his emails. After all, he rationalised, he could then give Verity advance notice of when to expect *Professore* di Stefano, the head of the University of Palermo's antiquities department.

Augusto glanced at his mother, who was loving all of it, utterly absorbed by Raimondo's peroration. Olivia smiled at Augusto understandingly. God, that man could talk! Finally Raimondo sat down to enthusiastic applause and beamed around the table. Gloria looked so happy surrounded by her family that Augusto almost forgave Raimondo.

CHAPTER 8

The love that dare not speak its name

Sunday

After a pleasant Sunday lunch at a trattoria overlooking the archaeological park, Crispin and Verity returned to their rooms to tackle the next set of letters. Before reading Barnabas, Crispin checked references to him in Luke's Acts of the Apostles in the Gideon Bible.

From Barnabas in Cyprus to Marcus Antonius Paulus in Antioch. Greetings

My beloved Paul, who brought me to know and love our Lord Christ Jesus as the prophesied Messiah and Saviour of mankind. I give G_d thanks daily for you and for the opportunity to serve Him in our shared ministry for so long.

I was greatly grieved at how we parted, with harsh words unreconciled. I know you had lost faith in John Mark, due to his deserting us earlier, but I felt he should be given another chance. Isn't the message of the Cross that, despite having sinned and fallen short of the glory of G_d, we can be restored into a righteous relationship with Him through G_d's abounding grace and our repentance? So, why were you not prepared to forgive our brother in Christ, John Mark? Your heart seemed hardened to his entreaties to continue sharing the Lord's mission.

I have often heard you say that we should respect those who labour among our brethren in Christ, that we should esteem them highly in love because of their work. Yet on occasion you yourself struggle to do this, if there are any points of disagreement between people. You urge us to be at peace with one another, yet you are never slow to engage in argument. You are quick to claim your authority as an apostle of the Lord and father in Christ to those whom you have drawn to Him, while dissembling from that claim. If you doubt me, I urge you to re-read the draft of your letter to Philemon. Sometimes asserting your authority is indeed for the sake of the Gospel of our Lord Christ Jesus, but at other times it appears to be more personal. You preach patience, yet are short tempered, and then become astonished if others take offence. Perhaps it is for the best that you never married, despite your pastoral advice to husbands as well as to wives.

Yet I miss you greatly. I will always be grateful to you for showing me the Way and I earnestly hope that I have not lost your friendship for ever.

John Mark and I worked our passage for places on a ship bound from Antioch to Cyprus. Never again! A storm blew up on the second day and I have never experienced anything like it. The waves were huge, crashing over the foredeck. The Captain had reduced sail to a minimum and made sure that everything that could be lashed down was lashed down. There were a couple of other passengers with us and, along with the crew, we had to take turns at pumping out the bilges just to stay afloat. All except me. I just lay in my hammock having thrown up until I was retching on nothing and wished that I was dead. I have never felt so ill. It just went on and on for hours and hours. I confess I prayed for the Lord to take me and release me from this horror. Finally the storm passed and we arrived safely, the ship having suffered some damage but no lives lost. A young sailor, no more than a boy, had broken his arm when the ship had lurched, suddenly throwing him

to the deck. He was in a lot of pain. John Mark and I laid
hands on him and prayed for his healing in the name of our
Lord, Christ Jesus. By the time we entered harbour his arm
was fully restored. Through this miracle we were able to
bring the Captain and some of the crew into sharing our faith.
How mysteriously G_d works for those whom he loves who
are called according to his purpose. Notwithstanding tavern
bed-bugs, I shall endeavour never to travel by sea again once
I have left Cyprus for the mainland.

I have grown increasingly close to John Mark as we have
laboured together for the Gospel. I cannot imagine working
without him. He is 'David' to my 'Jonathan' and, as is written
in our scriptures by the prophet Samuel:

*The soul of Jonathan was knit to the soul of David, and Jonathan
loved him as his own soul. … Then Jonathan and David made a
covenant, because he loved him as his own soul. And Jonathan took off
the robe that was on him and gave it to David and his garments, even
to his sword, and to his bow, and to his girdle.*

Give our greetings to all our siblings in the Way. May our
Lord give you peace at all times. The grace of our Lord Jesus
Christ be with Silas and all of you.

Your brother in Christ, Barnabas.

With shaking hands and moist eyes, Crispin put down the
letter. This was no academic text, but seemed to be speaking
directly to him. He realised that he loved Hilary more
than his own soul. He could no longer live a double life,
constantly dissembling to his parents and making excuses as
to why they couldn't meet him. The risks Barnabas took for
the sake of the Gospel were far in excess of those he himself
would have to encounter. (Unless of course the ancient

documents were found in his and Verity's possession before they had managed to return them.) He started to sweat at the thought. Yet even this alarming prospect could not shake his growing resolve. In spite of his compromised position he experienced a sense of clarity and peace that he had never felt before. He and Hilary could live openly and to *hell* with the consequences. Another emotion welled up inside him – joy. He felt freedom and *joy*. Free to live life in all its fullness, and joy at the prospect of an uncompromised future. He turned to God in prayer. Was this OK? Lord, is this from you? Please speak, I am listening.

The joy and sense of peace remained.

★ ★ ★

Crispin knocked on Verity's door, 'Hi, how's it going?'

'Fine, I'm some way through Prisca's letter to Paul. She's giving him quite a hard time actually. How about you?'

'I've just read Barnabas'. It drifts dangerously off-message from the Church's official attitude to the gay thing. Barnabas claiming he loves John Mark as King Saul's son Jonathan loved David, as much as his own soul.'

'How do you feel about that?'

'Actually it's strengthened my resolve to come out to my parents, so at least I can be true to myself and to Hilary. I think I've found the nerve not to lead a double life from reading this letter. How's Prisca coming along?'

'I'll bet that Barnabas letter will never get out of the Vatican. Prisca will also touch some tender points,' said Verity. 'Listen!'

From Prisca, wife of Aquila in Ephesus, to Marcus Antonius Paulus in Jerusalem. Greetings

I never cease to give thanks to G_d for our meeting in Corinth, when we had so cruelly been expelled from Rome with our fellows in the Way and all the Jews by the Emperor Claudius. Aquila and I lost everything we owned, our house, land, possessions and business. Praise be that we met you so he could join you in your tent-making operation. The welcome we received from others who recognise Christ Jesus as our longed-for Messiah was overwhelming. That which we have lost does not begin to compare with that which we have gained by this companionship of worship, prayer and service.

I have here a copy of the letter you wrote to our brothers and sisters in Corinth. There is a passage in it of such beauty that I reproduce it so that you may understand better what I am trying to say later on in this letter.

If I speak in the tongues of men and of angels, but do not have love, I am a noisy gong or a clanging cymbal. And if I have prophetic powers, and understand all mysteries and all knowledge, and if I have all faith, so as to remove mountains, but do not have love, I am nothing. If I give away all my possessions, and if I hand over my body so that I may boast, but do not have love, I gain nothing. Love is patient; love is kind; love is not envious or boastful or arrogant or rude. It does not insist on its own way; it is not irritable or resentful, it does not rejoice in wrongdoing, but rejoices in the truth. It bears all things, believes all things, hopes all things, endures all things. Love never ends. But as for prophecies, they will come to an end; as for tongues, they will cease; as for knowledge, it will come to an end. For we know only in part, and we prophesy only in part; but when completion comes, the partial will come to an end. When I was a child, I spoke like a child, I thought like a child, I reasoned like a child; when I became a man, I put an end to childish ways. For now we see as if in a mirror, dimly, but then we will see face to face. Now I know only in part; then I will know fully, even as I have been fully known. And now faith, hope, and love abide, these three; and the greatest of these is love.

This shows that you truly understand the love that we should have for G_d and for our neighbour and how that should play-out in practice. As you wrote to the Galatians.

For as many of you as were baptised into Christ have put on Christ. There is neither Jew nor Greek, there is neither slave nor free, there is neither male nor female; for you are all one in Christ Jesus. And if you are Christ's, then you are Abraham's seed, and heirs according to the promise.

'Copies of Paul's letters must have had wide circulation for Prisca to have read these, which were sent to far distant churches,' commented Verity.

'I suppose the churches exchanged them, even though some seem to have been addressed to very specific people and situations and cannot have been meant as general rulings. The risk is that those who have determined doctrine have expanded individual exhortations into overarching principles, rather than using a generalised moral framework to inform specific circumstances. In other words bottom up rather than top down. This can produce some seriously skewed results, especially in the subjugation of the powerless by the powerful.'

Paul, I appreciate how you have updated the household codes for families who follow Christ. Traditional Roman ones give extensive instructions to wives and children, while permitting the man to behave as he wishes. He would have the power of life and death over his entire household. However, your analogy of Christ being head of his Church as a husband should be the head of his wife breaks down in reality. Christ is perfect in every way and gave his life for the Church. Alas, husbands may be far from perfect, just or even reasonable and, to insist on wifely obedience in all circumstances implies that you potentially sanction injustice and violence. I know this is not what you meant and, with the imminent return of the Messiah, we cannot overthrow all the injustices of our current society. However, it will be taken by some as a licence to bully and abuse their families, conveniently forgetting that they should honour their wives as Christ honoured the Church. I quote some of the letter you wrote to us in Ephesus to make my point:

Be subject to one another out of reverence for Christ. Wives, be subject to your husbands as you are to the Lord. For the husband is the head of the wife, just as Christ is the head of the Church, the body of which he is the Saviour. Just as the Church is subject to Christ, so also wives ought to be, in everything, to their husbands. Husbands, love your wives, just as Christ loved the Church and gave himself up for her, in order to make her holy by cleansing her with the washing of water by the word … In the same way, husbands should love their wives as they do their own bodies. He who loves his wife loves himself. For no one ever hates his own body, but he nourishes and tenderly cares for it, just as Christ does for the Church, because we are members of his body.

And, as for that letter you wrote to Corinth, I quote:

As in all the churches of the saints, women should be silent in the churches. For they are not permitted to speak, but should be subordinate, as the law also says. If there is anything they desire to know, let them ask their husbands at home. For it is shameful for a woman to speak in church. Or did the word of G_d originate with you? Or are you the only ones it has reached?

How carefully did you consider the wording of that passage? You have affirmed women's ministry in all matters, both in writing and in speech. You have recognised that the Word of G_d may be prophesied by women as well as men. I am certain that you meant this comment to refer to interruptions in services which can occur if wives ask about the meaning of scriptures in which they have not been instructed. We are rarely offered the same level of education as you men. Do you realise that it is being used by your churches to silence the voices of women in church completely? Can you bear to have the words you've written twisted by knaves to make a trap for wives? Paul, you really must be more careful in how you express yourself! Often when reading your letters one can almost hear you striding up and down while dictating, without the benefit of prudent editing. The letter you wrote the Galatians is a prime example. In future do please craft them carefully so they cannot be misrepresented by the powerful to oppress the weak. That is not the message I know you wish to transmit.

As there is neither Jew nor Greek, slave nor free, male nor female, but all are one in Christ Jesus, for heaven's sake make sure what you write is consistent with that. You acknowledge that the lady Junia was an apostle in Christ before you, and therefore senior to you in the Church. I know how much you have benefited from Phoebe's wealth and high social position, and how you value that Lydia runs her own textile business. I know you are not trying to reduce us women to the subservient status of Roman women, so please don't write anything more that could be interpreted like that. Some Church leaders are now preventing well educated-women teaching men or having leadership roles in the churches, even ones founded in their homes! They call it 'Sacrificial Male Headship'.

That phrase brings to mind the beheading of our dear brother John the Baptist. Not what they have in mind, obviously. They insist that it means that men are always supposed to hold spiritual authority over women. What a twisting of the truth! Paul, you must write again, and this time please make it clear. Women and men are of equal value in Christ Jesus. One baptism takes us into Christ's own body where what counts is our love and our gifts – not whether we are male or female.

Aquila and I and all the saints send you blessings in the name of Christ Jesus our Lord.

'I can't see this one escaping from the Vatican either,' said Verity.

CHAPTER 9

The letters

Monday

Following breakfast, Verity and Crispin settled down to tackling the final batch. They were highly conscious that they only had today to work on them, check their transcriptions and translations, photograph the plaque and the scrolls, and re-roll them so that they would fit back into the chest and show no signs of having been tampered with.

> From Rabbi Gamaliel in Jerusalem to Marcus Antonius
> Paulus (also known as Saul) in Caesarea. Greetings

This is my sixth letter to you on this vexed subject of whether Jesus could be the Messiah and if truly G_d has raised him from the dead. In my last one…

'Hang on, where's letter number five?' asked Crispin.

'I'd hoped you'd have it, are you sure it's not got muddled up with the others?'

'No Verity. I've now only got Mama's and that one from Barnabas.'

'How maddening! I wonder what was in that one?'

'We can't worry about that now, let me see how this one goes on.'

In my last one I couldn't get beyond the earthquake you caused by your sentence:

For G_d has done what the law, weakened by the flesh, could not do, by sending his own Son…

What do you mean here by 'Son'? I know holy men are referred to at times as sons of G_d but we know that G_d is ONE. We say it in our prayers daily. Hear O Israel, the Lord our G_d the Lord is ONE. I realise you cannot have meant this figuratively, given your context and my head almost exploded. When I collected myself, I visited John, who was visiting Jerusalem. His confirmation of your seismic sentence was shattering. He led me back to the first verse of our scriptures.

In the beginning God created the heavens and the earth. And the earth was without form, and void; and darkness was upon the face of the deep. And the Spirit of God moved upon the face of the waters. And God said, Let there be light: and there was light.

John than talked me through notes he was keeping in order one day to write an account of who Jesus was, why he came, what he did while on earth, how those actions each signalled his true identity, leading on to how he died, how he was raised from the dead and what it all means for the world. His writing style is quite unlike yours, straightforward, clear Greek, but the ideas are ethereal. He allowed me to copy out a few short passages so I could study them and see how what they say is consistent with your (it must be admitted) rather dense description of what must be the most significant moment in G_d's dealings with us since the Exodus, if not the Fall.

In the beginning was the Word, and the Word was with G_d, and the Word was G_d. He was in the beginning with G_d. All things came into being through him, and without him not one thing came into being. What has come into being in him was life, and the life was the light of the cosmos. The light shines in the darkness, and the darkness did not overcome it.

He was in the world, and the world came into being through him; yet the world did not know him. He came to what was his own, and his own people did not accept him. But to all who received him, who believed in his name, he gave power to become children of G_d, who were born, not of blood or of the will of the flesh or of the will of man, but of G_d. And the Word became flesh and lived among us, and we have seen his glory, the glory as of a father's only son, full of grace and truth. The law indeed was given through Moses; grace and truth came through Jesus Christ. No one has ever seen God. It is God the only Son, who is close to the Father's heart, who has made him known.

John is emphasizing that, in the beginning was the Word, and the Word was with G_d, and the Word was G_d. He was in the beginning with G_d. And the Spirit of G_d moved upon the face of the waters. The Word of G_d spoke creation into being infusing it with his Spirit. The Word of G_d became a human being, Jesus, and can be called the Son of G_d in his earthly guise.

'Do you realise,' said Crispin, 'that this is the earliest example we have of the beginning of John's Gospel? The final version is normally dated to around AD 90. This must be at least thirty years earlier. John added in some bits about John the Baptist, but this part of the text is almost unaltered.'

I am speechless and I don't know what to think. That boy, if it was the same Jesus, that boy asking me about Abraham's three visitors at the oaks of Mamre. 'Who is this three-in-one Lord?' Am I to believe that unknowingly at twelve he was asking about himself? I realise that he must have grown into that belief of who he truly was. I heard reported that when the High Priest Caiaphas put Jesus under oath saying, 'Tell us if you are the Christ, the Son of G_d!' he responded, 'It is as you said. Nevertheless, I say to you, hereafter you will see the Son of Man sitting at the right hand of the Power, and coming on the clouds of heaven.' His reply was of course alluding to the prophecy of the final judgement given by Daniel hundreds of years ago. Then Caiaphas screamed 'Blasphemy!' Such a claim can only be blasphemous, unless it is true.

I remain at a loss of what to make of all of this. I send you greetings from Peter in Jerusalem. May you be blessed and kept safe by the Lord our G-d, who is One.

Your concerned teacher, Gamaliel

'This is dynamite,' Crispin exclaimed, 'but we really can't be caught with them. How on earth are we going to get all these rolled up and back into the chest unseen?'

'Rolling them up will be fine, and we'll have the transcripts by then. Thank God for St Cecilia giving us an extra day. As for getting them back, I'm sure we'll think of something.'

In fact, Verity was beginning to feel a lot less sure. As she'd feared, the scrolls had bulked up with the humidity and might not roll back neatly. Fortunately, the carbon-black gum ink was unlikely to smudge; however, the chest had been pretty full when they opened it and she desperately hoped that they would all fit back in. The disintegrated case for the bronze plaque just couldn't be helped.

'Crispin, don't you think it is quite a coincidence that the priest's sermon considered complementarity of the beginning of Genesis and of John's gospel and this letter does too? Twice in two days. I had such an extraordinary experience in that church and I keep getting tingling sensations with these letters from Gamaliel.'

Crispin grinned at her. 'Do you think God might be trying to tell you something?'

★ ★ ★

Verity went to check her emails, a reflex habit in between almost any action. There was one from Augusto.

'Augusto writes that the head of the antiquities department at Palermo University, Prof. Michaele di Stefano, will be coming to see him as soon as he can tomorrow. If we don't get to the chest and replace these before he arrives all hell will break loose. We should photograph them all now. I brought my father's single-lens reflex, as I thought we might need something better than my phone to take pictures of the catacombs. Perhaps you could hold the scrolls open here where the light's good and I'll shoot them. We ought to do them in the order in which each batch appears to have been written, ending with Timothy.'

'Fine, there's just one we haven't read together yet from Paul's mother, let's do that first. Then you can load them onto your laptop and perhaps email them to both of us, although to keep the detail they'll be around two megabytes each, so that will take some time.'

From Bernice, widow of Marcus Antonius Lucius residing
in Tarsus, to Marcus Antonius Paulus c/o The Emperor
Nero, Rome Greetings.

My Darling Sauli

I do hope that this letter reaches you. I have heard such terrible things concerning you from Phygelus, who has recently returned to the province of Asia from Rome. In prison! In chains! Oh my poor Sauli. Can you not renounce these silly notions about this Jesus being our promised Messiah? As I have said before, he can't possibly be because he is dead and nothing has happened. If anything the Romans are getting increasingly angry with the Jews in Jerusalem. I fear they may do something drastic, but what does a poor ignorant woman like me know?

I miss you so much. You have been away so long. My heart bleeds for worrying about you. My headaches are increasing both in length and severity. There is also another piece of sad news. Perhaps I should not tell you, but you are still the official head of our household. Livia married Joshua, the miller's son. Eli arranged it all. But it is so sad, I weep every time I think of it. See, you can see my tear stains smudging the ink. She became with child shortly after her wedding and we were all so delighted. The pregnancy went smoothly following the first three months, when she was very sick. Just before the baby was born we all became worried. It had ceased to kick inside her. Three days later she went into a terrible labour lasting a full day and night. Finally she gave birth to a boy, but the Lord had taken him from us before he had even arrived. Livia haemorrhaged greatly and, being so weak and knowing her first born son was dead, she gave up the ghost. We are all inconsolable.

My Sauli, I do so fear I may never see you again. I don't know what Abba would think of you. Have you discussed your ideas with Rabbi Gamaliel? He seemed such a wise man and I know you held him in high esteem.

I have nothing left to live for.

Your grieving mother, Bernice

Verity and Crispin remained silent for some time. 'Look, you can see the tear splodges,' he said.

Sombrely they laid out the letters in order on Verity's bed and started to roll them up. The moment any was released it unravelled into loose coils. In frustration Verity said, 'I'll nip down to the pharmacy, which with any luck will be open, even if it is a semi-holiday here, and try to buy some hair clips or elastic to secure them till we've got them all back in the chest.'

'Would you like me to go?' offered Crispin.

'No it's fine. See you in a bit.'

CHAPTER 10

The Cardinal

Monday

The Cardinal removed his reading glasses and rubbed his eyes, stretching stiffly in his gilt and brocade chair. He was a well-built man, whose formerly athletic body had fleshed out. He had a strong, handsome face, which had caused many a woman to wish that he had not taken a vow of celibacy. His closely cropped grey hair and steel-rimmed glasses added to his air of authority.

In front of him was a pile of letters requesting permission to inspect documents in the Vatican Archives. Normally his assistant would assess these, but he was away on a spiritual retreat. His secretary had removed the obviously bonkers ones. Why did they favour green ink, capital letters, multiple underlinings and obscure mathematical calculations? He was left with the mostly rational. Not for the first time he cursed the popular author, Dan Brown. In his blockbuster, *Angels and Demons*, his protagonist, Harvard so-called '*symbologist*' Robert Langdon, attempts to foil a plot to destroy the Vatican, hatched by a secret society called the Illuminati. He does this partially by finding documents in the Vatican Archives. Although, after careful vetting, scholars had for years been allowed to study much of the archive material, this damn book had boosted applications exponentially. They had had to take on more staff, just when the current Pope was keen that all available funds should go towards the alleviation of poverty and the spread of the faith.

It didn't help that the Cardinal had always lived comfortably, as evidenced by his girth and luxuriously appointed apartment. And now, at this time in his life, he was confronted with a frugal Pope.

Everyone, it seems, loves a conspiracy theory, and the Vatican had set itself up for tsunamis of them by being compulsively secretive and paternalistic, not to say authoritarian. Since the Vatican Bank and child abuse scandals, the Cardinal grieved that no one believed anything the Church said. The Pope, by his humble demeanour, simple lifestyle and outgoing personality, was doing much to counter negative perceptions but, alas, there was too much truth in the suspicions for even this Pope to ameliorate all the accusations. Ireland was a case in point. In one generation, faithful churchgoing and declared Christian belief had fallen dramatically. Films like *Philomena*, highlighting the systematic abuse of young pregnant girls and their children, who were taken in and split up by religious institutions, did nothing to help. Especially as the Vatican continued to cover up the historic activities of the Church.

The Cardinal put yet another request to look at the papal papers dating from 1939 on the NO pile. That was during the pontificate of Pius XII, who was accused of collaborating with the Nazis in aiding the extermination of Italian Jews. All that correspondence had been kept secret and would remain so for as long as possible. Also, what business was it of anyone to look at the personal papers of cardinals from Mussolini's rule onwards? Those always got turned down.

There were some real gems in the Vatican Archives, which did occasionally see the light of day, not all of them reflecting well on that institution. For example, there were documents from the trial of the astronomer Galileo and a papal bull excommunicating Martin Luther. The Vatican received numerous requests to study fourteenth-century documents relating to the trials of the Knights Templar – no doubt material for yet another hysterical historical novel.

Regular accusations of cover-up also surrounded the Dead Sea Scrolls, most of which the Vatican didn't even have. The Cardinal wondered what ancient documents might still be preserved in Eastern Orthodox monasteries. Maybe some in Coptic, that ancient Egyptian language written in the Greek alphabet? Some of those might well date back to the beginnings of Christianity. The monks, though they could not read the script themselves, were very reluctant to allow scholars to study them. This was hardly a surprise, as they had so often been deceived in the past and had had valuable documents stolen. With the current instability in the Middle East leading to the expulsion and murder of hundreds of thousands of Christians, perhaps these documents, if they existed, would be lost forever. Either way, now would not be a good time for new revelations, which might inflame further religious sensibilities. The Cardinal wondered if any new finds of first-century documents relating to Christianity would ever be made.

Reluctantly – he turned to the next batch of begging letters. This was more like it – requests to see correspondence between the papacy and some of the most famous people in European history: the Holy Roman Emperor, Charlemagne; the theologian Erasmus; the composer Mozart; the consummate artist, sculptor, military architect and poet Michelangelo; Queen Elizabeth I of England; the French playwright, Voltaire; and even Adolf Hitler.

The most spectacular looking document, housed in the reinforced concrete 'bunker' in the midst of fifty miles of shelving, was a parchment from England, complete with eighty-three signatures supported by eighty-one official seals dangling from red cords, asking why the Pope was taking so long to annul Henry VIII's marriage to Catherine of Aragon.

There was a knock on the door and the Cardinal's chaplain put his head round. 'I'm off to evening Mass. Are you coming today, Your Eminence?'

The Cardinal glanced up, smiled, placed a priceless renaissance bronze statuette as a paperweight onto the 'not-yet-decided' pile, snapped on the top of his gold fountain pen, got up and left.

CHAPTER 11

Opening the chest

Tuesday

On Tuesday morning, a group assembled at the entrance to the catacombs, half of whom were excited and half terrified. Verity and Crispin still had not determined exactly how they were going to get the scrolls and plaque back in the box without their theft being discovered. Just as Giuseppe was about to unlock the catacombs, a black Mercedes purred up. Verity felt her flesh crawl. Cesare emerged alone and went through his usual effusive greeting ritual, treating Verity to another hand-slobber, which she only managed to endure though supreme self-control. How on earth were they going to get rid of all these people and get a clear run at the chest? Verity had taken full responsibility and had the key and scrolls in her bag. Crispin was looking after her laptop in case she needed it. She had thought about how to delay Augusto, by having the chief executive of the Poghosian Foundation phone him on her mobile and insist on speaking to him then and there. She had not divulged to her employers the existence of the scrolls, but thought that the hole in the wall and the chest would be sufficient material for a lengthy conversation. She had expected that the CEO would have rung by now, which added to her anxiety. As they walked through the ruined church down to the catacombs, her phone rang. After a brief exchange, she handed it to Augusto and indicated that the CEO would also like to speak to Cesare. But how to deal with Giuseppe and Marco? Giuseppe, fortunately, had to contend with an electrical problem. Some fuses had blown, plunging the tunnels into darkness. Verity glanced appealingly at Crispin, indicating Marco. She needn't have worried.

'Marco, could you just show me that Roman sarcophagus you mentioned while Giuseppe gets the lights back on? I have a torch.'

Crispin and Marco peeled off down a side tunnel and disappeared from sight. There was no time to lose. Torch in trembling hand and soaking in sweat, Verity hastened down towards the chest. All was as they had left it. She hoped she would be strong enough to lift the lid. Feeding her bag before her Verity crawled through the hole in the false wall. She ended up having to hold the torch in her mouth, as there was nowhere else to put it. She was furious with herself for not having swapped torches with Crispin. Inserting the key in the lock, she prayed for the first time in almost twenty years. The key turned. Taking a deep breath she grasped the edges of the lid and heaved. It seemed stuck. She tried again. Nothing. Then the lights came on at the end of the tunnel. With a supreme effort she lifted the lid, tipping it back enough for it to stay open. Unfolding the linen, she placed the bronze plaque at the bottom in the fragments of its bag and laid the scrolls onto another layer of linen. She then carefully cut each of the elastic bands with which they had managed to secure them, systematically pocketing each one. Finally she placed the letter from Timothy on top. She and Crispin had done their best to re-roll the scrolls back to their original size, with variable results. At least they still fitted. She kept thinking that she might have left fingerprints, despite mostly wearing gloves and assiduous wiping. Why would anyone test for those? Well, they just might. Footsteps approached and she heard Cesare's voice. She gently lowered the lid, which made what sounded to her like a hideous clunk. Locking the chest, she slid the key under it just far enough in for it to be invisible. Finally able to take the torch out of her mouth, she wiped away the saliva dribbling down her chin. She then edged back though the hole as Augusto and Cesare approached. She hoped the latter wouldn't try and squeeze through it, as he would almost certainly increase the damage. Fortunately Cesare had no intention of dirtying his impeccable suit by scrambling about.

'I have asked Giuseppe to bring one of the masons to help take out the chest. They will bring it to my office,' announced Augusto.

At that moment Crispin and Marco returned. Crispin glanced surreptitiously at Verity and was relieved to see her level gaze. Marco seemed a bit out of sorts.

Giuseppe managed to lift the chest on his own and position it by the hole, through which it could be slid. As he stood up, he saw the key.

It was late morning by the time the chest had been transported to the office, by which time Michaele di Stefano had arrived from Palermo to examine their find. Coffee was served and Verity found herself munching through the amaretti biscuits to relieve her stress. Augusto's entire staff, including the gardener, had crowded into his office for the grand opening. Having second thoughts regarding the size of the audience, Augusto ushered all his staff, apart from Marco, out of his office. The last man slammed the door in annoyance. Maria stood alongside Cesare as Augusto reluctantly handed the key to di Stefano.

Di Stefano put on white cotton gloves taken from several pairs placed on the conference table. Augusto checked the temperature and humidity of the room in order to avoid any undue environmental shock to the chest's contents when, whatever it was, was exposed to the air. Not exactly laboratory conditions but that couldn't be helped. This was far too enticing a prospect for all of them to leave attempting to open it until the chest got to Palermo. Di Stefano gingerly inserted the key in the lock and, much to his astonishment, it turned first time. He then attempted to lift the lid, struggling with its weight. He heaved, and it creaked open, revealing the linen cloth.

Verity and Crispin didn't dare catch each other's eye but both were praying that nothing would be found amiss. They were aware that Oscar-winning performances of nonchalance, amazement, and excitement, at all the right moments, would now be required of them.

Di Stefano gently folded back the first fold of linen and gazed at the flat papyrus sheet. Verity glanced around the room. Augusto appeared to be trembling with excitement and was clearly itching to get his hands on the chest's contents. Marco looked equally enthralled, having managed to position himself close to Crispin. Maria was gazing out of the window into the middle distance, tapping her foot. Despite her feelings of revulsion, Verity looked across at Cesare, whose eyes seemed to glitter with avarice. He caught her gaze and winked lasciviously. She glanced away hurriedly, turning her attention back to the chest.

Hardly daring to handle it, di Stefano haltingly read out Timothy's explanatory letter, translating from the Greek as he went.

> To Reuben, Elizabeth and all the Saints in the church in
> Syracuse, from Timothy, Apostle to our Lord
> Christ Jesus. Greetings

I am sending you this casket for safekeeping. It contains letters received by our dear brother Paul, along with some of his effects, as I know you love him well. I hope to join you later in the year. The sea captain to whom I have entrusted this casket is in the Way.

We have a sure and certain hope of eternal life though the death and resurrection of our Lord Christ Jesus.

May the Lord bless you and your households.

Your brother in Christ, Timothy

There was silence as everyone in the room digested the document's potential significance, were it to be genuine. Laying it to one side, di Stefano gingerly unwrapped the next layer of linen, revealing the scrolls. Both Verity and Crispin scanned them, desperately hoping they looked untouched. With trembling fingers, di Stefano lifted up the top left hand scroll and read the text on its outside.

From Rabbi Gamaliel in Jerusalem to Marcus Antonius Paulus (also known as Saul) in Caesarea. Greetings

The room remained in shock.

Augusto exclaimed, 'This is the find of the century! It is unbelievable! That such treasures should be found here in Syracuse! I must tell the Vatican immediately!'

Di Stefano, the consummate academic, and also keen not to let events spiral out of his control, introduced a note of caution. 'This is potentially so amazing that I think we should examine them properly before any announcement is made. News of these findings should not leave this room until I have been able to investigate further.' He suddenly looked puzzled. He realised that the scroll was much more loosely coiled than he expected, as he found he could unroll it without resistance. Any ancient papyri he had previously encountered couldn't be unwrapped without steam treatment.

'This is most unusual. It is impossible to unroll such papyri without reintroducing humidity. They must be forgeries.'

'Perhaps the lead seal was so tight that it retained all its moisture?' ventured Verity.

All eyes turned to her and she felt herself blush. 'The wall behind which they were hidden could be dated once the fresco is revealed and pigment samples taken,' she added hurriedly.

Di Stefano nodded, acknowledging her logic. He picked up a scroll on the lower right-hand side of the chest, which unrolled equally as easily as the first. He frowned, struggling to read the text.

To her horror Verity saw that a knotted piece of elastic was peeking out from the edge of a recently disturbed scroll. It screamed out at her, although no one else seemed to have noticed it.

Di Stefano broke the silence. 'This is not in Greek. I can't read it.'

At the very moment that all eyes turned to him, Verity deftly extracted the elastic.

By this time Verity, Crispin, Augusto and Marco had all donned cotton gloves in the hope of handing the scrolls. Di Stefano handed the one he couldn't decipher to Augusto, who also frowned in puzzlement and then, reluctantly, handed it to Verity. He was secretly relieved that she couldn't read it either. Bypassing Marco she gave it to Crispin, and then focused her gaze firmly on the chest in order not to reveal her feelings.

After a tactful interval, Crispin announced, 'It's Aramaic.'

From Bernice, widow of Marcus Antonius Lucius residing in Tarsus, to Marcus Antonius Paulus in Corinth. Greetings

Both di Stefano and Augusto looked impressed and Marco pressed in a little closer to Crispin.

Verity decided she had to take command of the situation. 'As the papyri are so pliant, why don't Crispin and I assist you,

Professor, in attempting to transcribe them over the next day or so, to help you determine their likely authenticity and what we should announce to the press. Augusto, it might be best if you delayed informing the Vatican until such time as you have a firmer handle on their likely authenticity. I will also hold back from letting the Poghosian Foundation know.'

Augusto appeared to agree, and ushered the others out of his office, while making sure that the three remaining had all the materials they needed.

Di Stefano was deliriously happy, like a small child let loose in a sweet shop. The moment he caught sight of the bronze hinged plaque he was so ecstatic Verity feared for his health. He appeared not to read any significance into the shreds of black fabric on which it lay, so entranced was he at deciphering the Latin.

As the possible significance of Paul's citizenship proof and provenance became clear to him, di Stefano could hardly breathe.

'Not a single one has been found intact before this. Did you know that?' he exclaimed. 'All have had their seals broken and I don't believe that one survives from this era of the Roman Republic, before the emperors ruled. The only ones I have heard of have been granted to auxiliary soldiers at the end of their service in the Roman army. This is unique!'

Verity and Crispin were caught in a continuous déjà-vu loop, trying not to transcribe too quickly. All three had agreed to translate sections at a time and share their results, rather than ploughing though each letter in a linear manner.

Lunchtime came and went. Sandwiches arrived. Di Stefano hardly touched his, in contrast to Verity, who attempted to manage her stress levels by munching.

★ ★ ★

Augusto couldn't wait. He was in enough trouble already. He placed a call to the cardinal in charge of the Vatican Archives.

Cesare and Maria returned to *Bella Donna* and plotted.

Marco sulked.

CHAPTER 12

Indiscretions

Wednesday

Verity decided to reconnoitre the catacombs, noting every major area of damage and their renovation requirements. The excitement of the discovery of the chest had blocked everything else out, but now it was time to be thorough and to attempt a reconciliation of some of Cesare's invoices with work achieved, although she wasn't holding her breath.

Leaving Crispin to continue assisting di Stefano, and armed with a plan of the catacombs, Verity set off down the main tunnel. She decided to go to the far end and then work her way back. The ground was beaten earth and the air was cool, with a faint musty smell. She passed tunnels branching off to her right and left, each of which would have contained many corpses in the past. There were also carved into the walls niche after empty niche. She wondered how many bodies the entire complex had held at its peak. The lighting throughout was third-world-standard wire and bare light-bulbs, the latter becoming more sparsely spaced the further she penetrated the tunnel. Giuseppe had only managed a temporary fix, so the damp-corroded fittings flickered. Verity passed an intricately carved stone sarcophagus, which must have weighed nearly a tonne. Its damaged lid was slid half open. She was pleased that it was also empty. Even so, the place had an eerie feel. A rat scurried past her. She jumped.

Reaching what appeared to be the end of the main tunnel. she retraced her steps, systematically marking on her plan where work was required. The lights buzzed and flickered ominously. Having reached a cross-tunnel, she turned left towards one of the ancient water silos which had been converted to early Christian chapels. Its conical roof formed a funnel, which curved sideways out of sight, thus providing some ventilation, but no light. The space contained huge, roughly-hewn stone sarcophagi. Leaving that silo though one of its five exits, she continued her work. The tunnel she chose led on to a couple more silos and then she reached a dead end. Attempting to retrace her steps, she hit another dead end. Verity was sure she had chosen the correct return route but in the gloom perhaps she had been mistaken. She could hear rats scurrying just out of sight.

Remembering the ancient Greek legend of Theseus in the labyrinth hunting the Cretan Minotaur, she wished she had used Ariadne's technique of unravelling thread to show her passage. Even some chalk marks would have helped. Fighting down panic by taking firm control of her breathing, she set off once again, but seemed to end up where she had been some minutes previously. All the silo exits looked similar and, as she could see from the plan, formed a network. By now she was completely disorientated. Verity sat down on a tomb to compose herself. The lights gave one last flicker and died.

Thank goodness I swapped mine for Crispin's head-torch she thought, and rummaged around in her bag. She found it, but fumbled. It clattered to the floor with a snap of plastic, its batteries rolling into the dark. Now what? she wondered. Well, the lights would come back on some time and eventually someone would come looking for her. Crispin knew her plans.

Time passed and Verity thought she might try to make her way out by keeping one hand touching a side wall. This was easier said than done, as the walls were uneven with scooped-out niches. She really had no idea where she was heading. She stopped and waited, having lost all sense of time. She regretted not wearing her diving watch; its luminous hands would have helped.

Suddenly she became aware of the sickly smell of cologne. Verity felt her scalp tighten with fear. The last time she'd smelt it she'd been face down, half suffocating on *Bella Donna*, struggling not to be raped. Another whiff. Freezing, hardly daring to breathe, she could now see a powerful torch beam bouncing off the edge of a limestone sarcophagus, and hear footsteps approaching.

'Verity, are your there?' Maria's voice sounded.

Verity breathed again. 'Yes, I'm over here, just round the corner.'

Maria came into view wearing another figure-hugging outfit and vertiginous heels. 'Giovanni mentioned you were here while he was struggling with the fuse-board, so I thought I'd come and find you. Are you all right?'

'Yes thanks, I'm fine. Could you just shine the torch down here? I've dropped some batteries.' They were swiftly retrieved, at which point the lights spluttered on.

'Would you like a coffee?' enquired Maria. She had heard rumours concerning the contents of the chest and was keen to quiz Verity about them.

'Yes, why don't we do that, there's Café Mauro just outside.'

Verity still felt shaken but allowed herself to be led out of the catacombs and Church, round the corner to the cafe, where she sat down and waited, until Maria emerged with two double espressi and some amaretti biscuits. She smiled her most sisterly smile at Verity.

'Augusto seems very excited by the chest and what seem to be ancient letters. Have you worked out who they're from or to?'

Verity hesitated. They had agreed not to divulge their

thoughts on the contents until di Stefano and Kairós could issue a joint press release. She was unaware that Augusto had cracked and, as they spoke, a Vatican representative was on his way to take control of the chest, its contents and the entire situation. As far as Verity was concerned, di Stefano was due to take the letters to Palermo tomorrow for laboratory testing. What harm could there be in telling Maria what they thought?

'It's very exciting. It looks like these are letters written to St Paul by his former teacher Rabbi Gamaliel, by Paul's mother and two of his companions, Prisca and Barnabas. There is a covering note from his protégé, Timothy, explaining that they had been sent to Syracuse for safe-keeping after Paul's martyrdom in Rome.'

'Does that make them very valuable?'

'To the world of scholarship, and to further our theological understanding, they would be priceless.'

'Yes of course, but if they were sold?'

'If these are what we think they are, they would never be for sale. Technically they are owned by the Church, as Kairós is a Vatican offshoot and they would never offer these on the open market.'

'Please tell me about them, they sound fascinating.'

Verity found herself explaining some of the contents of the letters. She found it a relief just to be able to talk about them. The strain of the last few days and her recent fright had eroded her normally highly-tuned judgement. Maria employed her full-force charm, effective not only on men. On describing Bernice's missives they both had a good laugh, despite the last one's sad ending.

'Di Stefano plans to take the chest up to Palermo tomorrow, by taxi, as he doesn't have his car here. I think he'll leave around 10.00 in the morning.'

Fully recovered, Verity returned to the catacombs to complete her survey armed with Maria's powerful torch, just in case.

★ ★ ★

Cesare stretched, luxuriating in a post-coital haze and listening to water lapping gently against *Bella Donna*'s hull. Maria was quite amazing and often surprised him with something new. This time she'd tied him up with silken cords and repeatedly teased him with a riding crop just short of his point of no return. She made the most of her black basque-encased body. Finally she released him and he flipped her over onto the coverlet, taking her from behind, as he preferred. Her creamy taut buttocks were accentuated by scarlet suspenders supporting fishnet stockings.

Lighting two cigarettes, he handed one to her. 'Now, what did you get out of Verity?'

Maria slipped on a silk gown and proceeded to relate their conversation. 'She said the letters, which is what they are, are priceless. She wasn't certain that they were genuine and not later forgeries but, given Augusto's and di Stefano's behaviour, I'll bet they believe that they're the real thing. She said they'd belong to the Vatican and that it would never sell them. She even implied that the Vatican might prevent others seeing them.'

'Priceless? So a private collector would pay top dollar.'

'You think Orlovsky?'

'Orlovsky! Maria, you are a genius. I was waiting for a suitable moment to give you this. Now is perfect.' Cesare went over to a wall-safe concealed behind wooden panelling. He brought out a flat, blue leather box embossed with gold. 'Shut your eyes.' Maria felt a heavy gold chain round her neck, which fastened with an expensive click. Cesare turned her to face the mirror. 'Now look!'

A spectacular purple amethyst surrounded by diamonds was suspended on a thick-linked chain studded with both jewels. Cesare kissed her neck. 'You are divine!'

Maria proceeded to show her appreciation in the best way she knew how. Yet she was not content. Who or what did Cesare's new mobile with the *Never on Sunday* tune signify? She must lose no time in secretly transferring funds.

CHAPTER 13

di Stefano

Thursday

Cesare had phoned di Stefano at his hotel offering to take him back to Palermo with the chest, rather than incur the cost of a taxi. Di Stefano's car was in the repair shop, having lost an argument with a bus, and he had come by cab. The office was deserted as Augusto and Marco were giving a presentation on Syracuse's history to some schoolchildren. Di Stefano carefully carried the chest downstairs and gently placed it in Cesare's Louis Vuitton trunk, which had been lined with foam for the purpose. The two men lifted it into the Merc's boot alongside some similar luggage and Cesare threw a tartan rug over everything.

It was late morning and, seemingly on a whim, Cesare suggested that they should take a detour and stop for lunch at a wonderful little restaurant he knew, run by a cousin of his.

'Simple you understand, nothing grand, but honest country food.'

Di Stefano remonstrated that they should get back with their precious cargo, but he was enticed by the attraction, courtesy of Cesare, of the sort of meal he could not normally afford. They left the motorway just north of Catania and drove up into the hills. The roads got narrower and dustier, and eventually they turned up an unmade track with a sign, 'Agriturismo'. A shaggy dog came bounding down the lane, barking, and then happily chased the car back up it. Grey stone walls appeared, within which was a large, open, iron-grill gateway. They pulled up at what appeared once to have been a farmhouse; adjacent barns and stables had been converted into holiday homes, with rustic stone walls, terracotta tiles and bottle-green shutters. These surrounded a pretty planted-up courtyard, in the centre of which stood an ancient well with a cast-iron pulley. Potted scarlet geraniums and draped purple bougainvillea along with oleander bushes softened the stone.

A comfortable-looking woman bustled forward, smiling and exclaimed, 'Welcome! Welcome! Lovely to see you again Cesare. Such an unexpected visit.'

'This is *Professore* di Stefano, an eminent archaeologist from the University of Palermo.'

'Delighted to meet you *Professore*, this way please. It is warm enough to eat outside, no?'

With the dog bouncing about, the *signora* led them onto a vine-shaded terrace overlooking a swimming pool, beyond which was an olive tree and a vine-clad valley. Glasses of prosecco and a little dish of herb-scented olives arrived. Di Stefano felt himself relax. This was flattering, and a delightful interlude from his rather dreary job in Palermo, though the potential of the letters kept raising his pulse and making him smile.

'What do you think of these letters?' asked Cesare. 'Could they be genuine?'

'They are more likely to be medieval forgeries. There was a great trade in relics, as they attracted fee-paying pilgrims, and letters to Saint Paul would have been revered. At first glance, the fresco behind which they were found looks early, but that has not yet been verified. Of course we'll have to do a range of tests.

'First, is the papyrus of the correct age, along with the ink? We will also carefully examine the chest. The elemental composition of the bronze and its lead lining will help to date it, along with carbon-dating of the wood. The chest certainly resembles those of that era. We have Roman chests that look very similar and its lock is either an excellent copy or it is genuine.'

He had Cesare's full attention.

The *signora* bustled back.

'My dear, today we have a wonderful rabbit stew, or some fish fresh from the boat, perfect for grilling. To commence I will bring some antipasti. Then, how would you like your pasta? With roasted vegetables, home-made pesto or clams?' She beamed at them.

It was going to be one of those lunches over which they would linger until late afternoon. Di Stefano was thankful he was not driving. Cesare indicated that he should choose. He opted for pasta with vegetables and the rabbit stew. His wife was not an adventurous cook. Cesare selected the same. At that moment the *padrone* appeared with a bottle of heavy, vintage, red wine, already decanted. He explained that he had opened it a couple of hours ago, as otherwise it would not be at its best. A nerve in di Stefano's gut twinged. This statement was not entirely consistent with Cesare's seemingly serendipitous suggestion of an impromptu lunch, but he instantly dismissed any qualms. It was all just too lovely. A dish of cured meats, gherkins, smoked cheese, artichokes and caramelised baby onions accompanied by freshly baked rough country bread appeared. Cesare was assiduous in replenishing di Stefano's glass. The tagliatelle was buttery, cooked to *al dente* perfection and lightly coated with chargrilled peppers, aubergine, onions, zucchini and tomatoes. Utterly delicious.

Cesare appeared to take a great interest in di Stefano's work. He sympathised at the poor pay and at the underfunded conditions in which he operated. He seemed to imply that he might be able to offer some assistance with the costs involved in dating the letters.

'It is not enough to establish that the papyrus and the ink are of the correct era,' di Stefano expounded. 'We have many palimpsests, documents where the original writing is erased and new material has been written over it. Papyrus was expensive, and so has on occasion been reused, confusing the dating of the final text. There is no attempt to deceive, it was just a practical solution to a cost problem. Using X-ray and other scanning techniques it is often possible to read the original script. The most exciting example is that of an old Orthodox prayer book which was found with Greek mathematics underlying it. It purported to show an analysis of calculating the areas under curves using fractional sections which are the elements of differential calculus. It was possibly written by our own Archimedes some 2,000 years before Isaac Newton.'

Cesare looked suitably impressed and topped up di Stefano's glass once again.

Di Stefano continued. 'My first impression of reading the letters in Greek is that they seem plausible. I cannot read Aramaic, but those from Gamaliel and Prisca, well if they're fakes, someone has gone to a lot of trouble and they do seem consistent with what we know from the New Testament and the Talmud about each of those people, as well as having acute insights into St Paul's theology.

'Regarding the rest, the linen wrappings can be estimated, though carbon dating is notoriously unreliable for linen. However, spinning and weaving techniques used over time and across geographies have been well classified – for example, the Shroud of Turin. Carbon dating conducted in the 1980s placed it in the fourteenth century, but the samples had been contaminated by the testers using fragments from its edges to minimise the damage. The samples were subsequently found to have been in regions where nuns in the sixteenth century effected repairs using cotton dyed to match the yellowed linen, thereby confusing the results. The Shroud's weaving is consistent with that from first-century Palestine, and pollen and limestone dust would also indicate a Near Eastern origin.'

'Do you think it could be the shroud of our Lord?' asked Cesare incredulously. He had not thought a scientist would buy in to what he had assumed was religious wishful thinking.

'It's hard to explain. The image is only clear when photographed, as if it were itself a photographic negative with the body as the light source. Then you see this haunting face and a body bearing all the marks of the passion: flogging, face beaten up, nose broken, crucifixion and a spear wound in his side. The image has a long pigtail down the back, which appears in no known painting of Jesus. An odd thing to invent. Another strange feature is that no pigments or dyes have been identified on it. Only the bloodstains, and these appear to have been applied before the image. Unusual, if it were a fake. The blood group is AB, which is more associated with the Semitic races of the Middle East than those of Europe. If a medieval artist created it on old linen, it is surprising that we have no other examples of this sort of work. It is quite beyond my ability to rationalise it scientifically.'

The rabbit casserole was rich, gamey and plentiful, accompanied by mashed potato to soak up the juices and a green salad. Di Stefano couldn't remember when he had last eaten such a good meal, and with such a sympathetic and assiduous host. He glanced at his watch: 3.45 – still enough time to get back to the department before it shut. Anyhow, he had the keys, but not to the most secure strong-room where precious objects were stored. But then, what could possibly happen overnight?

The woman bustled back, looked appreciatively at their empty plates and said, 'Speciality of the house, tiramisu.'

There are many recipes for tiramisu, all of them delicious. The word means 'pull me up'. The story is that a madam of a certain establishment found that some of her clients were having a little difficulty in the performing department, so she concocted a dessert whose ingredients would assist matters: coffee and sugar for energy, eggs and mascarpone cream cheese for stamina, Marsala wine to get in the mood, all soaking sponge fingers and with a dusting of cocoa powder. Di Stefano reckoned he would need to be entirely pulled up after this lunch. With the tiramisu came limoncello, a dessert *digestivo*, tangy with lemons. Cesare excused himself briefly, hovering out of sight near the espresso machine. Di Stefano pocketed a business card of the restaurant. Maybe he would come this way again.

Coffee arrived, and then Cesare finally suggested they should be moving. Bidding everyone expansive thanks and farewells, they drove back down the rutted lane and eventually resumed their motorway route to Palermo.

★ ★ ★

Verity and Crispin sat at Café Mauro discussing what she should put in her progress report to Poghosian. Developments had taken a spectacular turn, but the renovations were no further on.

'I must tell them what we think has been found but of course they may be medieval fakes and I don't want the whole thing to blow up,

'You don't actually think they're fakes, do you?' asked Crispin.

'No of course not, I'm sure they're genuine but we still have to be careful not to know more about them than di Stefano has deciphered. Augusto is very excited as he hopes that this will raise the profile of the catacombs and, even if they can't keep the originals here, they could exhibit facsimiles.'

I can see a whole new building project looming,' said Crispin, 'Perhaps using a different contractor?'

Verity smiled.

Crispin continued, 'Should you send Poghosian some photos? By the way, have you downloaded them yet? I'd like to have a copy before they have copyright slapped on them. If they are ever published, that is,

'No, I keep meaning to, but I haven't got round to it yet.' The fact was that Verity was feeling increasingly possessive about the images and didn't feel ready to share them or to have them on too many platforms; just in case. 'I plan to do a thorough search of the catacombs and compare the original specification and quote with results thus far. Could you then mark up the plans for me?'

At that moment the two mothers with their children appeared again. It was becoming a regular spot for all of them. Crispin again looked at the children wistfully and wondered.

★ ★ ★

Di Stefano drifted into a doze. Before they reached the outskirts of the city, Cesare pulled over into a service station, leaving di Stefano sleeping deeply. He patted himself down, pulled out one of his phones and speed-dialled. Engaged. He frowned and waited, keeping an eye on the car. Some ten minutes later the old imperial Russian national anthem sounded. These days it was only heard as part of Tchaikovsky's *1812 Overture*. A tense conversation ensued involving hard bartering. Both sides were accomplished negotiators. A deal was struck. Cesare then refuelled the car for appearance's sake and continued his journey, making quite sure that they would not arrive before the department was locked up for the night.

Drawing up outside, Cesare groped in the now unconscious di Stefano's pockets until he located some keys. Rohypnol was a wonderful drug. On waking, the archaeologist would have no recollection even of the lunch. Two men who had been parked in a side street with a view of the door slipped out of the shadows. They saluted Cesare and, as he unlocked the department's front door, they effortlessly carried di Stefano up the steps, laying him down on the reception area's black leather sofa with his briefcase acting as a pillow. The Louis Vuitton trunk was placed just behind the reception desk. Replacing the keys in his pocket meant that they couldn't re-lock the door, but that was not their problem.

Cesare and the men drove in convoy to the private yacht section of the docks, into a lock-up warehouse and unloaded Cesare's luggage. One of them then set off in the Merc back to Catania. Cesare and a crew-member carrying the luggage boarded *Bella Donna,* which growled off into the night.

★ ★ ★

Early the following morning di Stefano awoke with a cracking headache and a mouth seemingly full of sour sawdust. He groaned and fell off the sofa. Totally disorientated, he attempted to work out where he was. Dim green lighting from two exit signs gave him a clue and he managed to make it to the toilet just in time. The last thing he remembered was being offered a lift back to Palermo. With a sickening lurch, panic seized his befuddled brain. Where was the chest? He stumbled around, and tripped over it. It was still locked. Relief flooded through him. He sat down and racked his brains over what could possibly have happened. At six he phoned his wife to tell her not to worry, that he had been held up and was in the department. She had been about to phone the police, as he had never stayed out all night before. Having doused himself with water from the cooler and drunk some of the caretaker's left-over coffee, he began to feel more human, if still stickily unwashed and unshaven.

The caretaker arrived, astonished to see him, closely followed by a couple of di Stefano's young colleagues, who were itching to see the chest and letters, of which they had only received hints. They carried the trunk into his office and di Stefano produced the key. He lifted the lid with a flourish and thought he would faint. Like a Russian doll, inside there was another, smaller Luis Vuitton chest. Lifting it out with shaking hands, di Stefano hesitantly opened the second case. Inside were house-bricks.

'Oh my God!' gasped di Stefano. 'Oh my God!' He mindlessly picked up and put down the bricks as if he could will the chest into materialising. 'It's gone, but how? I know I saw the letters in the chest and I locked them in this case myself. Here is the key. Oh my God! What can we do?'

'Should we phone the police?' ventured one of his colleagues.

'Yes. No. I don't know. What can I tell them? The chest. It must have been stolen. But how?' Di Stefano's head pounded and all he could hear was roaring in his ears. He slumped into a chair, putting his head in his hands.

'Sir, I really do think we ought to call the police, as the longer we leave it the more time the thief has to get away.'

Di Stefano moaned, 'I suppose you are right, go ahead then.' His colleague went to an adjacent office and picked up the phone.

Surprisingly shortly afterwards two *carabinieri* arrived.

Di Stefano was shaking violently now, and quite incapable of giving a statement. One of the officers asked him to empty his briefcase. Unconcernedly, di Stefano fetched it and handed it over. A zipped-up inner compartment contained rolls of high denomination euro banknotes.

'I have never seen those before! They are not mine! I must have been drugged and robbed.'

'Sir, traditionally robbers remove money *from* their victims,' the policeman remarked drily.

Di Stefano's voice rose to a falsetto. 'No! I mean the chest and the letters have been stolen and this money has just been put in my briefcase to frame me!'

'Really? You will please accompany me to the station. None of you is to touch anything. My colleague will stay here until we can remove the trunk.'

'But I am innocent. I have been robbed and framed!'

'Come along sir. That is for the magistrate to decide. Do you have a lawyer?'

* * *

The group of islands, of which tiny Lampedusa is the largest, is Italy's most southerly territory, 109 miles from Sicily but only 70 miles from Tunisia. It has become a destination of choice for those seeking asylum in the European Union, being closest to the eastern North African and the Middle Eastern coasts. There have been many scandals of overloaded rust-bucket boats with insufficient fuel and no life-jackets foundering before arrival, losing all hands on board. If the boats are intercepted, or if survivors are picked up by the Italian navy, they have ended up in appalling conditions in holding camps, but at least they are not massacred.

People-trafficking had become a big, well organised and

profitable business. Cesare had prospered in it, especially after the recession had hit his building trade. There were two streams. There were those who genuinely wanted to claim asylum, and had to pay in full up-front. On arrival they surrendered themselves to the Italian authorities. Then there were those who came to better their life prospects. They could be loaned the money by traffickers and stayed on their books. Cesare operated a cell network around the troubled coasts so that, even if one cell was caught by the authorities, they couldn't spill contact details regarding another cell, let alone the organisation as a whole. The cells each had a 'boat-finder', a victualler, and a couple of middlemen who would offer transport to the desperate.

Cesare tried to segregate the passengers into either one or the other type per trip, but it was not always possible. Before they were released to the authorities, asylum-seekers were held back until the others could be secreted away. Cesare then moved the economic migrants to Naples, one of the busiest ports in the world, where container ships load and unload twenty-four hours a day. The bulk of this cargo was perfectly legitimate, with many Chinese exports to Europe first landing there. However, there was also a highly profitable parallel trade in illegal drugs. Cesare was not in the drugs business, as he had an unspoken agreement with the Mafia *capos* that he would not try to carve out a slice of their business, provided he could use some of their distribution networks to facilitate trafficking people. His involvement stopped when he received payment at the port. If the economic migrants couldn't raise the cash sum required (and provided they survived the journey and avoided arrest), they would become indentured workers for years in order to pay off their passage – the men in menial labouring jobs, the women often coerced into prostitution. Deductions for food, clothing and accommodation often put their passage price out of reach indefinitely. If they travelled with identity documents, these were confiscated by the traffickers.

Bella Donna, with its precious cargo, sped towards Lampedusa. Cesare had an excellent relationship with the port authorities, who accepted the odd stuffed envelope and absented themselves when required. He also had some very secure buildings in a remote valley.

CHAPTER 14

Holland Park

Thursday

Sergei Ivanovitch Orlovsky kissed the icon of St John, crossed himself and then sat down. His senses were suffused with the smell of incense, with candlelight glinting off gilt, and with the solidity of the ornately carved arm of his chair, complemented by the heavy folds of dark velvet around the walls. In front of him stood a large gold and jewel-studded crucifix, which had once adorned a pre-revolutionary Russian Orthodox church. He allowed himself mentally to float, engaging with the numinous. Time had no meaning. He seemed to bathe in a sea of tranquillity.

Priceless icons were housed in niches and a heavy, pierced-brass hanging lamp gave off a diffuse light. This was his private chapel. He had a regular arrangement with the priest from the Orthodox Cathedral, Knightsbridge, to come and give his family Holy Communion.

The chapel doubled as the family's safe room. It could be sealed off from the rest of the house, with independent air-conditioning and water supply. Behind some of the wall hangings were fold-up beds, food (and vodka) stores, a bathroom, extensive communication devices and a gun cabinet stocked with unlicensed automatic weapons.

Orlovsky was a second division and second generation oligarch, who had picked up mining, steel, cement and aluminium assets from some of the disgraced first generation as they fell foul of the Putin regime. He had stayed out of active politics but made sure he remained on good or at least neutral terms with as many factions as possible. Still, you never knew – hence the Holland Park apartment, formed from two, grand, stucco-faced houses, laterally converted. The foreign rich don't like stairs. His wife loved living in London and the children could be safely escorted to school by just one member of staff. He still owned property in Moscow and a *dacha* in the country, but he based himself here. Despite the security benefits, he found exile hard. His soul was rooted in Russia with a romantic emotionalism which got the better of him after too much vodka.

Aristocratic backgrounds were never boasted of these days. The Revolution had swept all those titles away, although he noticed that Count Tolstoy used his title in London as did Prince Obolensky. The Orlovskys had once been aristocrats with huge tracts of farmland, hundreds of serfs and a place at court. His great grandfather, Count Nicolai Orlovsky, in a seemingly rash act of teenage rebellion, joined the young revolutionaries in Moscow in 1917. He jumped the right way, lost all his lands and titles but managed to save his family, most of whom fled to Paris. Unfortunately, Nicolai chose to stay and so his family lived through the Soviet era on the less comfortable side of the Iron Curtain. Sergei had been determined to restore the family fortunes and had done so in spades.

Unusually, Orlovsky retained a deep personal faith. His elderly grandmother, his *babushka*, who had been a young girl during the Revolution, had imbued in him a love of God and the conviction that God loved him. He had been christened Sergei after St Sergius, a fourth-century Roman soldier who, with his colleague Bacchus, was martyred on discovery that they were Christians. Sergei's personal morals and business ethics were no longer all those his *babushka* might have wished, but the trappings of religion definitely helped him connect with the cultural heritage he had left behind. He collected religious relics and treasures.

Orlovsky was a fair, thick-set man in his early forties, beginning to run to fat, with high cheekbones and dark, almond-shaped eyes betraying some Tartar ancestry.

He had first encountered Cesare when they part-exchanged cement plants, as each had one in a location more convenient to the business interests of the other. Over a celebratory dinner, Orlovsky had described his passion for Church treasures. Shortly after this, Cesare had found him a renaissance altarpiece which had adorned a side chapel in Palermo Cathedral, and which had been removed during early twentieth-century restoration work, and forgotten about in a cellar. Orlovsky had chosen not to enquire too closely into its provenance, nor how Cesare had managed to obtain it.

Earlier today he had had this extraordinary phone call regarding letters that might have been written to St Paul. Would he be interested? Would he just! He realised that he could not wait for them to be verified as genuine. This would be his only opportunity to obtain them, so their price would represent the multiple risks in so doing and perhaps discovering them to be fakes. He had not thought through how he could do that without attracting attention, but getting hold of them was his priority.

Could he trust Cesare? Clearly these letters were not legitimately his property but he seemed certain that he could deliver them. Both men had the sort of contacts who could mete out swift and brutal revenge if either considered themselves to have been double-crossed. He would transfer no meaningful amount of money until he had the chest and its contents. Maybe 10 per cent to show good faith? To be cheated by some Sicilian peasant was unthinkable!

He entered a reverie. How would it be to handle letters

which St Paul had held and read? Letters written by attested New Testament figures – Rabbi Gamaliel, Barnabas and Prisca? He would be just one degree of separation from his hero, Paul. His heart raced and he broke into a trembling sweat. To touch what Paul had touched! To read what Paul had read! To know what Paul had known! Maybe he would be granted divine insight into holy matters? And Paul's mother, what would she have written? Could one tell from her letters what sort of woman she was and what sort of man Paul might have been?

He rose and went to a niche where an icon was displayed. 'AGIOS PAULOS' were the words written either side of the head of a short, bandy-legged, bald man with eyebrows meeting in the middle. He lifted it off its stand and raised it to his lips, then reverently replaced it.

CHAPTER 15

Confession and absolution

Augusto sat at the head of his office table with Crispin on one side and Verity on the other. His face was ashen, and held the expression of a condemned man who could hear the firing squad loading their weapons. In a barely audible whisper he announced,

'The chest and letters have been stolen.'

Silence suffused the room as they tried to take in his words. Verity looked at Augusto aghast. She had known something was wrong when Giuseppe had hurried down to bring her and Crispin up from surveying the catacombs. The tension was broken by the arrival of espressi. Verity mechanically ate all the biscotti.

Finally Crispin asked, 'What happened? Didn't di Stefano take the chest to Palermo?'

'I thought so. That was the plan. Di Stefano has had a mental breakdown and a complete memory loss as to what happened. One of his staff just phoned me to say that he found himself in his department first thing this morning with what looked like the case in which the chest had been placed, but it was full of bricks.'

Verity snorted, although it wasn't really funny. It seemed such a cliché; bricks substituted for treasure, in this case for priceless papyri.

'Di Stefano has no recollection of how he had got to his department, having woken up there early this morning. He's lost almost 24 hours. He recognised the outer case but thought he must have arrived in a taxi. Marco is checking with all the local firms.'

'Where's di Stefano now?' asked Verity.

'He's in police custody with a doctor in attendance. They found thousands of euros in his briefcase, but none of his preliminary transcripts.'

'I assume he was set up,' said Crispin, 'but no one could sell the letters, not on the open market anyway. The provenance of the chest would be less of a problem.'

Augusto hung his head and shook it slowly from side to side. All his hopes had crumbled into dust. He was a broken man. Verity struggled to take in the enormity of the loss. Also, how careful she and Crispin would have to be about admitting what they knew of the contents. They could become prime suspects. After all, they had a better grasp of the significance and likely authenticity of the find than anyone else.

Mental images of the Kirchner murder-suspects handcuffed in court flicked across Crispin's mind, as he thought along the same lines. What if their rooms were searched and the transcripts were found before they could provide a plausible explanation of how they'd got them. If the letters could be 'borrowed' by them once, why not twice? And the pictures on Verity's camera? The two of them were hugely implicated. I always considered it was madness to take them, he thought. Maybe we'd better leave for home immediately; however, extradition within the EU was probably straightforward.

'What will you do now?' asked Verity.

'I had previously been in touch with Kairós in Rome and the head of the Vatican Archives is on his way down to take custody of the find. He should be here any moment. I am ruined.'

Verity and Crispin glanced at each other. Clearly the Vatican had wasted little time in getting its hands on their discovery. Though not quite fast enough in this instance.

Augusto gestured weakly and the two of them took their leave. Once back in Verity's hotel room they considered their options.

★ ★ ★

The Cardinal sat in Augusto's office at the head of the table, with Augusto twisted to face him. The Cardinal had put to one side the rollercoaster of emotions he had experienced on hearing about the scrolls, their possible provenance, and then their disastrous disappearance. Augusto's job, reputation and entire future hung by a thread. A thread the Cardinal held. He considered that adopting a pastoral persona would be the most conducive to evincing the truth. 'You had better tell me everything from the beginning.'

'I am so sorry, just so sorry. I don't know how all of this can have happened.'

'I understand, my son. Perhaps we can start with the grant application.'

'You know how difficult it is to get renovation grants these days, with the Italian economy still on its knees. We were having to close off more and more of the tunnels in the catacombs, as they were deemed unsafe, and we began to get poor reviews on TripAdvisor for the dingy entrance, pitiful levels of information, old-fashioned faded brochures and visitors complaining that we were not good value for the ticket price. The Poghosian Foundation came as a godsend. They specialise in religious renovations, as you know. I think the current chairman's Armenian grandfather made a vow that if his family should escape the Ottoman genocide, he would dedicate his life to the promotion of the Christian faith through art. They also commission new religious artworks.'

'Yes, I am aware of the excellent work they support,' interjected the Cardinal. 'Do continue.'

'Having been successful in our grant application, I put the building works out to tender. You know what it is like here in Sicily. If a building firm is not controlled by one Mafia clan, it is part of another.'

'So you chose the one who does not seem to have strong Mafia connections. Was that the only reason you selected Cesare Romano?'

The Cardinal's avuncular tone undermined Augusto's last reserves. He cracked. All the strains of the last few months and, especially, the last few days, now became too much. He started to sob. The Cardinal hid his distaste at seeing a man so reduced and offered him a large, monogrammed handkerchief. Augusto pulled himself together and haltingly explained his obligation to Cesare, his sister's illness and medical treatment, how he had hoped it would turn out all right, how there had been unforeseen difficulties but also some imaginative invoices, consuming the grant. The discovery of the fresco had also put them behind schedule. As the Cardinal listened patiently, his pastoral instincts, long buried under administrative obligations and high-office, began to emerge. He once again experienced Jesus' compassion and forgiveness for a repentant sinner. His ability to identify with the broken was what had originally drawn him into the priesthood. Years of political manoeuvring and stultifying ritual had smothered it, but embers of empathy remained, now to be rekindled.

Eventually, with occasional recourse to the handkerchief Augusto recounted the departure of di Stefano with the chest. He, Augusto, had not been around when di Stefano had left and, somehow, no one had seen him go. It was known that the archaeologist would have had to get a taxi back to Palermo, but requests to the local firms had yielded nothing. As the Cardinal was aware, di Stefano had been found in his department with rolls of cash, no ancient chest and amnesia. He had been released from police custody into medical care.

'Oh, Your Eminence, can you ever forgive me? I have been so foolish. I had just hoped it would be all right and now we have this disaster on our hands!' Augusto's head was bowed in mortification; his shoulders slumped and his fingers twisted the handkerchief round and round.

The Cardinal's heart was moved. 'Yes you have been foolish, my son, and you have paid a heavy price for it. I shall ask our Saviour to forgive you and together we will try to rescue this situation. Before we continue, is there anything else you would like to confess before Almighty God?'

Augusto paused, and couldn't think of anything except that he hated his wife's brother, Raimondo, so he confessed that.

The Cardinal placed his right hand on Augusto's head and said, 'Almighty God, who forgives all who truly repent, have mercy upon you, pardon and deliver you from all your sins, confirm and strengthen you in all goodness and keep you in life eternal.' Then, using his right thumb he made the sign of the cross on Augusto's forehead. 'May the blessing of God Almighty, Father, Son and Holy Spirit be with you now, and always. Amen.'

'Amen.'

Augusto straightened up, his eyes moist with gratitude. He now had a glimmer of hope and a powerful ally. Maybe all was not yet lost.

'Who else knows of this discovery?' asked the Cardinal.

'I imagine half of Syracuse once Giuseppe had been round the bars. There are no secrets here for long.'

The Cardinal looked pensive. 'The chest itself is of some value, as it is most likely to be Roman, but the scrolls? No one could publish them unless they could prove their provenance.

Like many stolen famous works of art, they are unsellable on the open market, but tend to be ransomed back to the galleries from which they were taken. The middlemen make tracing the perpetrators almost impossible. But what could be done with these, even supposing they are genuine?' He paused in thought. 'One does hear of secret hoarders who will buy up treasures just to have them in their vaults. These days, that seems mostly to be the Chinese. You remember those priceless Chinese jade artefacts that were stolen in 2012 from the Fitzwilliam Museum in Cambridge? The thieves were caught and jailed but the treasures were never recovered. It is assumed they are now in China. Could we be dealing with something like that?'

Augusto looked blank. He didn't want to think the unthinkable; that the scrolls would be lost before they had even been properly transcribed and read.

★ ★ ★

When di Stefano's wife had taken his suit to the cleaners, she had found a restaurant card she didn't recognise. She went immediately to see Michaele at the clinic, and as soon as she handed the card to him, it was as if scales fell from his eyes. The restaurant! The meal! Their drive! Cesare and the chest. Piece by jumbled piece the sequence seeped back into his consciousness. There were gaps, certainly, but enough returned.

'I must phone Augusto!' he exclaimed.

'Shouldn't you phone the police?' she responded. 'You're still under suspicion and are effectively being kept a prisoner here.'

'You said the head of the Vatican Archives has come down? He will know what to do and he will have contacts the police can never match. Augusto can put me through to him. I must speak to them now!' he shouted.

Alarmed by the noise, an orderly entered. 'Is everything all right?'

'Yes, yes, I remember what happened! I must speak to Augusto now!' di Stefano insisted.

The orderly glanced at di Stefano's medication schedule and checked his watch.

His wife said, 'He is sane! We have an urgent and private telephone call to make and my mobile gets no signal here.'

'I will ask the director if you can use his office.' He returned shortly, and accompanied them along several corridors and up one floor. 'Dial nine for an outside line.'

The director, intrigued, sat by the open-line extension in his assistant's office.

★ ★ ★

The two men gazed at each other as Augusto replaced the receiver. 'Cesare has them.'

'Cesare! He must have a buyer or he wouldn't have taken such a risk. We don't have much time. Tell me all you know about him: what he wants, what he fears, what his aspirations are. How would he like people to perceive him? What would he like his legacy to be? What motivates him now?'

Augusto took a deep breath, hugely relieved that some action could be taken. 'I think he has so much money that more wouldn't be an incentive. Anyhow, it might be hard to outbid the sort of buyer he must have.'

'You think that the Vatican could be outbid?' The Cardinal checked himself. Under previous regimes, of *course* not, what with them owning their own bank. But now? With this frugal Pope? Trickier.

'Personally Cesare has a reputation as a lecher and he's clever. He did his best to prevent Verity and Crispin finding out about the catacomb renovations. However, he may have overplayed his hand, as she became ill on his yacht. The call I received from Crispin stated that Cesare was not to be present during our next meeting. Maybe something happened? Our gardener heard rumours; he's related to the taxi driver who picked her up from Cesare's yacht and drove her back to the hotel.'

Augusto continued, 'Fear of assassination and falling foul of rival organisations is always present in his world, but Cesare is clever and has thus far managed to avoid feuds; at least to stay out of those which turned lethal. I think he wants status, public recognition. He no longer wishes to be seen just as a possibly illegitimate poor boy who made good. He wants the sort of official recognition money cannot buy.'

A slow smile spread over the Cardinal's face. 'Now that is something the Church certainly *can* supply.'

CHAPTER 16

Cardinal's move

Cesare and the Cardinal sat opposite one another on a soft white leather banquette in the saloon of *Bella Donna*. Each knew that they were to play a high-stakes game. They were not to be disturbed.

'Again, I cannot say how honoured I am to have such a Prince of the Church on my humble boat, Your Eminence.'

'The pleasure is all mine, Signor Romano. I get to the coast far less often than I would wish. There is something so refreshing about the sea.'

Not the most brilliant of opening gambits, but this game would stretch them both.

'*Signor* Romano …'

'Please call me Cesare, Your Eminence.'

'Very well, Cesare, Augusto tells me that you and he were at primary school together.'

'Yes. Both our families went there. His sister, Olivia, still teaches in the village.'

The Cardinal noticed Cesare's eyes soften at the mention of Olivia. Maybe his feelings for her were an opening? He smiled avuncularly. 'Olivia, did you know her well?'

A wistful look crossed Cesare's face. 'We were close once but our lives went different ways.'

'Not completely though. I understand you were very generous towards the family when she became ill? Augusto must have been grateful.'

At once Cesare sensed a trap and realised he must play this game with more of a poker face than he had done thus far.

'They were almost *family,* and one should always support the family, no?'

'Almost family? That would have had nothing to do with you winning the tendering process for the catacombs restoration project of course?'

'No certainly not! Augusto is a man of the highest integrity and would never confuse his professional responsibilities with personal obligations.'

'Obligations?'

'What I mean it that my company offered the best deal on a fixed-priced contract. There were many unforeseen events once we'd started. Tunnel collapses, the difficulty of moving stone sarcophagi from narrow tunnels where no machinery could be used, and then the fresco. The costs spiralled.'

'I imagine it was an awkward time for Verity Hunter to arrive, checking up on the work and the accounts.'

Cesare's poker face was put to the test.

The Cardinal gave Cesare a measured look. 'She had lunch here on your yacht I understand, but had to leave suddenly having been taken unwell, though no one else suffered from food poisoning.'

He knew! Damn he knew! But there was nothing he could prove. Anyhow the silly girl might have enjoyed herself, if she'd allowed herself to. She needed a really good seeing-to. What else did the Cardinal know? Cesare's mind buzzed.

'These women, such delicate stomachs. Perhaps the lobster was too rich for her. I do not find her *simpatico.* She is very serious, always working with that boy Crispin. He is rather "delicate", if you know what I mean?'

The Cardinal's mouth twitched. The Church was liberally furnished with 'delicate' men who loved dressing up in lace and robes while enacting the high drama of the Mass.

'The fresco slowed everything down, though I still had to

pay my men. We have also had to rewire many of the tunnels, which was not part of the initial quote.'

'Yes of course,' the Cardinal soothed. 'I quite understand. Then there was the discovery of the chest filled with papyrus scrolls. which tragically has disappeared. If they were indeed letters to St Paul, as di Stefano has suggested, they would be of inestimable value to the Church and to scholarship.'

'I know nothing about their disappearance; I am as mystified as anyone as to where they could have gone. Who could do such a thing with holy relics and how could one sell them?'

'Quite,' purred the Cardinal. 'However, we are both men of the world. You, maybe more of this world and I, perhaps more of the next, but between us I sense we might be able to find both the scrolls and a beneficial outcome for all concerned. In the course of your, er, *professional operations*, you must be very well connected. Perhaps you might enquire of your contacts if they can offer any clues as to the whereabouts of this chest. Not only I but His Holiness would be most grateful. He has authorised me to offer to the person who could lead us to the chest with its contents intact a papal knighthood. The Order of St Gregory the Great. This man would become a *Cavaliere*, of whom there are not many these days in Sicily.'

Cesare knew all about the Order of St Gregory the Great. It was one of the five Orders of Knighthood of the Holy See, and was an honour awarded to persons in recognition of their personal service to the Holy See and to the Roman Catholic Church. It had four classes, of which Knight/Dame was the entry level. Recipients of the Order included Governor General Sir Peter Cosgrove of Australia, the conductor Ricardo Muti, Otto von Habsburg, the last Crown-Prince of Austria-Hungary, football manager Matt Busby, boxer Henry Cooper, entertainer Bob Hope, the British politician, Ann Widdecombe, who converted to Roman Catholicism when it was ruled that women priests could be ordained in the Church of England and, most controversially, Sir Jimmy Savile, who has been posthumously accused of multiple sexual assaults on minors. The Archbishop of Westminster has requested Savile's annulment.

There was a long pause. The silence was broken only by the faint rumble of the auxiliary engine. The Cardinal sat motionless. Would Cesare take the bait? Could he, the Cardinal, close the deal? Suddenly the muffled clanging of the 'Anvil Chorus' intruded. Cesare fished out the phone and switched it off. Mama would have to wait. He looked over at the Cardinal, who appeared impassive. Cesare calculated that if he double-crossed Sergei Orlovsky the latter would be furious and dangerous. These Russians have a long reach, even to Sicily. But so had the Church for that matter. He decided to play for time.

'I could make some enquiries, Your Eminence, but I am uncertain where to start. I know that one or two of my contacts have business arrangements with fine-art collectors. I could begin with them.'

'The Church would be most grateful if you would try. We might also be able to help with fleshing out your fixed-price contract. Complete all the work you have contracted to do for Kairós and send the invoices, *reasonable* invoices, direct to me at the Vatican. This will prevent the Poghosian Foundation being reluctant to work for a Church organisation again.'

The Cardinal took his leave, Cesare's Mercedes having been placed at his disposal to transport him to the residence of the Archbishop of Syracuse.

From pawn to knight. The Cardinal hoped he would not be rooked.

CHAPTER 17

Bella Donna

Maria and Cesare had dined well on the *Bella Donna,* which was now powering back to Catania from Naples. There they had rendezvoused with the Cardinal and a posse of *carabinieri.* In a discreet handing-over ceremony, Cesare relinquished the chest and received a thick cream envelope embossed with the papal coat of arms. It contained an invitation to an audience with the Holy Father some two months hence, where Cesare would be installed as a Knight of the Order of St Gregory for services to religious and historical culture. A further sheet contained colour illustrations of the order – an eight-pointed star with St Gregory on the obverse and the motto *Pro Deo e Principe – For God and Prince –* on the reverse, suspended from a watered silk scarlet ribbon with gold edge stripes. The holder was also entitled to wear a dashing bottle-green uniform with a black beaver and ostrich-feather cockaded hat, the ensemble completed by a pearl-handled sword. Cesare had already planned an appointment with his tailor. He had finally arrived, *Cavaliere Romano.* That sounded *so* good.

He hadn't yet thought how he would square things with Orlovsky. Clearly he would have to repay his deposit and he must find a nice relic for him as compensation. He hoped Orlovsky wouldn't miss too badly what he had never had.

There was a slight chop to the sea as the wind whipped foam off the wave crests, which glowed phosphorescently in the moonlight. Maria took her cognac out onto the stern deck. She loved being at sea with the motion of the yacht as it sliced through the waves and the tangy salt spray, even if it did mess up her hair. She stood by the flagpole looking back at the receding lights of Naples. The ensign streamed, cracking in the wind.

Maria was troubled. Recently Cesare had taken more calls from the phone with the *Never on Sunday* theme tune and always disappeared out of earshot. Her heart burned with jealousy and she was determined to discover who this woman (and she was sure it must be a woman) was. She fixed a tracking device to Cesare's Merc, which fed its location back to her phone. A particular village outside Catania was a regular destination. While hating herself for doing so, she plotted. The next time Cesare said he was off to a business meeting in Catania, Maria was ready. Borrowing her cousin's Fiat, her head cocooned in a scarf and anonymous dark glasses, although it was not particularly sunny, she gave him some forty minutes start. On a winding lane she managed to hit roadworks. The man on the hand-held Stop/Go sign seemed to be in a trance on *Stop*. Her stress levels mounted. What if she didn't get there in time? She hooted, which caused the sign holder to look at her lazily and make a rude gesture. This never happens to me when they can see my face, she thought, but now was not the moment to unveil herself. Finally he twiddled his pole to *Go*. Spinning her wheels on the loose chippings, she zipped past and continued towards the village. Her phone told her that Cesare's car was still there. It was two o'clock and the high street was all but deserted. The shop was closed until five pm, the bar was open and two old men could be seen dozily playing cards through the doorway. Siesta time. Most of the houses were small, terraced, lime-washed in soft terracotta, but a bit higgledy-piggledy in design. Some of their shutters were freshly painted and some badly in need of repair. A cat lazed on a doorstep, looking superior. Maria drove past the church and edged through some badly parked cars, wondering how the Mercedes had managed, if indeed it had. Over the brow of the hill the road widened, and newer, more substantial houses appeared on her left, while the older terraces continued along her right.

Here! According to the tracker, it should be right here. She drove forward slowly glancing around and hoping she was not drawing attention to herself, despite the fact that no one seemed to be about. Curtain twitching is a universal small-neighbourhood phenomenon. No sign of the car. Maria continued until she reached the end of the village. The tracker indicated that the Merc was now behind her.

Turning round, she edged back the way she had come and, glancing through some closed wrought-iron gates, past a child's tricycle and toy tractor, she just saw the three-pointed star badge, which looks so like a gun-sight when driving. Maria turned left into a side street and parked, enabling her to see the gates in the rear-view mirror. Killing the engine, she waited.

Feelings of humiliation and shame assailed her. She felt a fool sneaking around like this but knew that she just *had* to know. It wasn't so much that she loved Cesare, but he was her escape from the ghetto and, if her role in bed could be usurped, what of her others? Maybe she was becoming less useful to him, in his mind at least. Time crawled by. Flies buzzed. An old woman dressed head to toe in black shuffled past on arthritic feet. She glanced at Maria but without much interest. A police car cruised down the high street. The gates remained closed. Then two young men on un-silenced motor cycles, with helmets dangling elegantly from their wrists roared down, the racket reverberating. That would be the end of anyone's siesta, Maria thought. She was too keyed up to do anything except focus on the gates.

Then, some movement. The gates opened slowly. A willowy, blonde young woman with Slavic features appeared, closely followed by Cesare. In full view they kissed passionately. Maria burned with rage and had to stop herself storming out of the car to confront them. The Merc nosed out and the two of them waved goodbye, before the girl turned and the gates silently closed. The irony, Maria thought: now Sicilians were able to employ eastern Europeans to look after their children, when in the past it would have been the Sicilians doing the domestic drudgery. Back in her flat she schemed. Self-protection and security were the keys. As the old saying had it; she'd been poor and she'd been rich. Rich is better.

Maria realised that time might also be running out for her on another front, which could be more serious, even lethal. She had been arranging the transfer of money from the so-called 'shipping' company into her new accounts. Money laundering laws had made moving large sums of cash around more difficult than it used to be, but she was a mistress of the black economy. Cash-based businesses as diverse as scrap metal dealing as well as building supplies, and second-hand vehicles to adult-entertainment clubs all played their part. Thinking she was alone in the office, she had left the door ajar while negotiating several deals. Just having finished a phone call, Volpe came in and, by the triumphant look on his face, he had overheard her last, highly compromising conversation sending the money to her personal account in Luxembourg. He said nothing – but now Maria knew he had something on her which could prove highly damaging. The two of them had never got on. Maria viewed Volpe as a nasty little man. He resented her sex appeal and the hold she had over Cesare, where once he, Volpe, had managed negotiations and client meetings.

No red-blooded Sicilian male would allow either infidelity or financial cheating to go unpunished. Were Cesare ever to find out that she had been siphoning off funds, her life would not be worth living, and indeed wouldn't be lived for very much longer.

What now? She glanced at the turbulent wake creaming away from the twin screws. They were making some twenty-five knots. She noticed that the sliding steel stern gate had not been drawn across and secured. Halfway through fixing it she stopped, slid it back and wiped her handprint from it with a tissue. Returning to the saloon, Maria handed her empty brandy balloon to a crew member and indicated to Cesare that she would go up to the bridge to have a word with the helmsman. Cesare smiled at her indulgently. It had been a good evening and he had high hopes for later.

Shortly afterwards Cesare himself went out onto the stern deck, which was slick with spray. The swell was increasing as *Bella Donna* sharply altered course, the waves striking her beam, causing her to roll.

No one heard the splash. By the time Cesare surfaced *Bella Donna* was too far for his shouts to carry. Having had a lot to drink, the shock of being immersed meant he didn't suffer long.

CHAPTER 18

Fire and brimstone

The convoy of *carabinieri* cars pulled away from Naples' private yacht harbour. The Cardinal was in the lead vehicle, the chest in the centre, with four heavily armed policemen taking up the rear. The transfer had been discreet and smooth, from the Louis Vuitton trunk to a bubble-wrap-lined plastic document box hurriedly bought from a stationery supplier. The Cardinal had checked its contents against a list provided by di Stefano and was confident that all was in order. As they snaked through the early evening traffic, the Cardinal allowed himself to relax. What could possibly go wrong? One never knew and everything was in the hands of God, but he felt he had done all that was humanly possible to obtain the optimal outcome. He thought back on his discussion with His Holiness. It had not been easy to persuade such a high-minded Pope to sacrifice what could be considered justice on the altar of expediency. However, he had managed to frame the situation as part of Divine providence that such significant documents should fall into the hands of the Church before they should either disappear forever or be exploited by the media.

He had assured Verity Hunter that as soon as was practicable scholars would be allowed to examine the scrolls, though he sensed she did not entirely believe him. She seemed to be more confident in his assurance that the work on the catacombs would be completed forthwith, with no further requests for funds from the Poghosian Foundation, to which of course the

158

Vatican was very grateful for its support of Italy's religious and historical heritage.

Verity was an impressive young woman he thought, totally on top of her job and remarkably resilient given what he suspected had happened on *Bella Donna*. However, he was puzzled at how she seemed to have an extraordinary grasp of what the letters contained, and he had caught her checking herself a couple of times when discussing them. Presumably she had only had access to them for the couple of days before di Stefano returned to Palermo? He was also puzzled as to how the scrolls had retained their flexibility, even though they had been in a lead-sealed box. Thank the Lord he had them now and, once they reached the A1 autostrada, it would only take some two hours to arrive at the Vatican.

★ ★ ★

Orlovsky woke with a racing heart and drenched in sweat. It took him several seconds to realise that he was safe in his own bed, in London, with his wife sleeping peacefully beside him. It had been a terrible dream. He was a young boy again back in the family *dacha* in the woods. The house was decorated for Christmas with ribbons, candles and stars. In the living room was a secret little tableau of the stable with Mary and Joseph, the baby Jesus, angels, shepherds and the Wise Men. All were beautifully painted wooden figures, along with an ox and ass. It was put away if they had guests, as it was not wise to be known as believing Christians. There was a fire burning in the grate and oil lamps shed a soft, smoky glow. His parents were visiting friends so he was alone but waiting with eager anticipation for his *babushka* to arrive with presents. In his dream he saw her riding in a sleigh through the woods and realised with mounting horror that she was being stalked by a pack of wolves. He shouted and shouted to warn her, but no sound came. He tried to run but couldn't move. The wolves closed in until the horses smelled them and bolted. The sleigh hit a rut, overturned and threw his *babushka* out. The horses in their panic dragged the sleigh along on its side. The wolves descended on his *babushka*.

He was wide awake now and thought it wouldn't do any harm just to check his emails. Flicking on his iPad, to his surprise he saw one from Romano Holdings. He had been expecting to hear from Cesare giving details of the chest handover and he had already transferred funds into an untraceable account. He had not expected Cesare to use an insecure channel like email. It contained no message but two attachments. He decided to risk opening them, doubting they contained malware. The articles in *Giornale di Sicilia* were about to change that view.

BUILDING BOSS DROWNS OFF YACHT

The body of multi-millionaire head of Romano Holdings, Cesare Romano, 58, was retrieved from the Straits of Messina late yesterday. He had been missing from his luxury yacht, *Bella Donna*, for three days. The skipper, Gianni Rosso, 36, has been bailed pending further police enquiries. It is alleged that the stern safety rail had not been secured. However there has been no suggestion of foul play. A company spokesperson, Maria Rizzi, who was on board at the time said, 'This has been an enormous shock to all of us in Romano Holdings. Signor Romano was an exceptional businessman, excellent employer and a good friend. Our thoughts and prayers are with his family at this sad time. His death will be a great loss to all who knew him.' His family at his €2 million villa were not available for comment.

Orlovsky absorbed the implications of the article. Of course it was very sad that Cesare was dead, and a tragedy for his family, but what about the letters? Where now was the chest and who might know about it? Maria was the obvious person with whom to start. He remembered her from the cement deal. What red-blooded man would not remember her? The situation might be recoverable. He opened the next attachment.

SECRET LETTERS TO ST PAUL IN FLAMES

Last night a catastrophic crash on the A1 northbound south of Rome closed the motorway for hours. Road works had narrowed the carriageway to one lane, slowing the traffic to a crawl. Despite warning signs, a fuel tanker ploughed into cars queuing in front of it and overturned, spilling gasoline across the road, which exploded into flames. Miraculously no one was critically injured. The tanker driver, who is now under arrest, is alleged to be Albanian and it is suggested that he had been driving for at least eighteen hours. Among the vehicles destroyed were three from the *carabiniere*. Everyone escaped before the spilt fuel erupted in flames, except one of the policemen who is in hospital suffering from burns but his life is not in danger. Witnesses claimed to see a man who had been travelling with the police wearing a scarlet skull cap.

Rumours have linked the convoy to information about a casket found in the Syracuse catacombs of St John the Evangelist. It was alleged to contain previously unknown first-century letters written to St Paul. Works foreman, Giuseppe Neri said, 'I found the chest behind a fresco in the catacombs. It contained papyrus scrolls, which the experts said were written to St Paul. Then a Cardinal came down from the Vatican, so I suppose they were important.' No one was available for comment either from the Vatican or from Kairós in Syracuse.

The Vatican's attempt at a press embargo had clearly not reached down to the Sicilian tabloids.

★ ★ ★

Verity and Crispin attempted to process the fact that the scrolls had perished. It seemed unbelievable. She had tried to talk to Augusto but he had shut himself away.

'This is a huge loss to scholarship,' said Crispin, 'theologically, doctrinally and socio-historically. It is mind-blowing to find an independent, non-Christian contemporaneous account of some of Jesus' teaching, his trial and crucifixion by Pontius Pilate, as well as the rumours surrounding his resurrection. Apart from the early Gnostic gospels, nothing has been found like this for two thousand years! It would seem to confirm that John, son of Zebedee, who was with Peter in Jerusalem, was the same as the writer of what is known as the gospel according to John. Also new is how Paul came to be a Roman Citizen and that he carried his authorisation with him, so he could always prove it. The fact that he was a citizen is why it was so shocking when he was beaten with rods by the authorities, something which wouldn't have happened to a Roman. Maybe he couldn't get to the plaque to prove that in time? I'm sure what di Stefano said was right, we have only got much later versions of those citizenship bronzes and all of them have been broken open, mostly with their seals missing, so what has been lost was unique.'

Verity added, 'Prisca's admonitions on how he referred to specific women in his letters and how the church took the individual incidents and made universal doctrine out of it clearly started early. Had this letter come to light in ancient times, maybe the patriarchal structure developed by the church might have been ameliorated, though I am not so sure. As for Barnabas and John Mark, that really was the "love that dare not speak its name".'

'I've sometimes wondered if that was also Paul's "thorn in the flesh"?' said Crispin. 'It seems clear to me to have been a moral rather than physical problem given how dismissive he was about his beatings, etc. These scrolls don't shed any light on that and any such suggestion would have the entire evangelical edifice come crashing down on your head.'

'Best not to go there then,' commented Verity.

Crispin smiled ruefully. 'Paul's mother's letters give a fascinating insight into his domestic situation and the fact that small-town scandals are much the same now as then. His citizenship thing is really interesting.

Thus they found themselves at a loose end. There was little more they could do in Syracuse and the earliest available flight home was not until tomorrow.

'We could go sightseeing,' said Verity, 'just like Cesare hoped we would. How about a trip up to Etna?'

'That would be interesting. I could compare it with Vesuvius, which I climbed when I visited Pompeii. It is safe, I assume?'

'Smoky but pretty safe I think,' responded Verity. 'Though it is an active volcano and erupts every ten years or so.'

'And the last time was?'

'They won't let us near it if it's dangerous,' affirmed Verity.

'Have you downloaded the photos onto your laptop yet?' asked Crispin.

'No, I keep meaning to, but somehow haven't got round to it.' Verity failed to add that she had become increasingly possessive concerning the photos and wanted to keep them to herself a while longer. She was terrified that her laptop and camera might be stolen, even if they were in the hotel safe, so she had kept her camera with her at all times. The Vatican had a long reach.

'Do you want to do that now? You could send them off to the Cloud as well.'

'Oh it'll be fine, we can just add some pictures of Etna. There's masses of space left on the memory card.'

'If you're sure.' Crispin wasn't convinced, but didn't want to press the point. It was Verity's show after all. He was just the catacombs specialist. However, he'd been brought up on the horror story of T. E. Lawrence leaving his first and only draft of his *magnum opus, Seven Pillars of Wisdom,* at Reading station while changing trains. The odd PhD thesis had been similarly lost before the advent of photocopying, let alone Cloud storage. He retained a niggling doubt.

Verity asked the hotel to arrange a taxi for the day, negotiating a flat fee. The trip to Etna was scenic and the volcano was in frisky form, spewing out fire, smoke and molten lumps of lava. It was forbidden to ascend it that day so they had to make do with some distant shots.

The two of them strolled down the street towards a trattoria that had been recommended for lunch. There were still some tourists milling around, most of whom had come off a cruise ship. Verity stepped towards the pavement's edge, to give space to a couple who looked as though they must inhabit the ship's twenty-four-hour buffet. She didn't notice the Vespa start up behind her.

Suddenly, her shoulder was wrenched as her camera was deftly grabbed by the scooter's pillion rider. It sped off, weaving through the traffic. Verity recovered her balance and started to chase it, immediately realising that it was pointless. She slumped onto a seat at a pavement cafe, shocked.

She couldn't bear to look at Crispin. How could she have been so stupid? It would only have taken a few minutes to back up the pictures, but she thought they were safe with her and that there would be plenty of time. The only photographic record of the papyri. Gone. They still had the transcripts, but those would be worthless without the originals as how could they prove they hadn't just made them up? Di Stefano could corroborate them, but his credibility had been thoroughly compromised by losing the scrolls and his transcripts in the first place. Conspiracy theorists would have a field day.

Crispin sat down next to her and prudently said nothing.

'I suppose we'll have to report the theft to the police. I don't imagine in a million years the pictures will be recovered, but at least I can claim for Daddy's camera on insurance,' mumbled Verity.

'Were we to make the transcripts public, we'd have to explain how we'd obtained them. That might be both our careers finished, certainly mine,' mused Crispin. 'Come on, let's get the police bit over, it could take some time.'

★ ★ ★

A couple of short, swarthy late-teenage brothers entered a bar in the back streets of Catania. Glancing around the almost empty room, they ordered two Peroni.

'Is Enzo around?' one asked the barman.

'He'll be here soon. You've something for him?'

'Might have?'

'Like I say, he'll be here soon.'

They sipped their beers, keeping a backpack firmly between them. Time passed. About to order another drink, they were interrupted by the entrance of a sharply dressed, carefully groomed, slender man sporting a multi-dialled Breitling watch.

'The usual, Piero,' Enzo tossed over his shoulder as he went into a back room. As he passed, he registered the brothers' presence without acknowledging them. His perch gave him a good view of the street, the bar and its back entrance onto an alley.

Enzo raised an eyebrow as the men approached him, one holding his *digestivo*.

'Something of interest, gents? I hope it's none of yer cheap rubbish you offered me last time. There's no market for that stuff. Y'know what I mean?'

'It's the real deal,' said one, fishing out from his bag a hi-spec digital Nikon SLR camera. Enzo examined it minutely. It did indeed seem to be the genuine Japanese branded kit and not a cheap Chinese rip-off.

'What d'you want for it?'

'What you offering?'

'€550.'

The brothers looked unimpressed.

'This is really good gear. We checked on the web. New, they sell for €2,000.'

'It's not new. You don't have the box, receipt or guarantee. It's certainly VAT free, unlike your web price. Tell you what, as it's you, I'll give you €650.'

The haggling continued, but Enzo held most of the cards. He was a reliable fence and always paid up, while never revealing his 'sources'.

As they parted, Enzo reminded them that there was a good

market for iPads, provided they could interfere with the tracker device.

'Keep taking the tablets,' he said as he strode out into the back alley, leaving them to pay for his drink.

CHAPTER 19

Homeward bound

'Cabin crew, please take your seats for take-off.'

Verity took out her phone in order to switch it off and saw a new email. Her heart gave a little skip.

guidoriccio.fogliana@sothebys.com. Hi Verity, you'll never guess. I've been promoted to head up Sotheby's Antiquities Department out of London. Coming over next week to check it out and will start the job next month. It would be great to catch up. Are you free for dinner Thursday? Hope to hear from you soon. G

They took off and made a slow turn. Verity looked out of the window to see the fields shrinking, the distant hills and the IKEA sign. She found herself silently chatting to God. Thanking him for having helped her sort out a difficult situation and now giving her something else to look forward to. Since her vision in the church she had had a secure sense that she was not alone.

Of course the loss of the letters was in one way disastrous. All that had been recovered from the shell of the burned-out police car was some melted bronze. She and Crispin had not yet decided what to do with the transcripts, which no one else knew they had. Without the originals or photographs, it would be impossible to prove that they were genuine and not just their inventions. It would also be tricky to explain how they had achieved them.

Crispin flicked through the airline magazine. His eye was

caught by a post-marriage interview with Elton John. In it he described how he and David Furnish had adopted their sons Elijah and Zachary and how happy and settled that had made them feel, as they were now a *real* family. Maybe, just maybe, he and Hilary could do the same? He thought Hilary would make a great dad and he had always liked children. It might assuage his mother's anguish at having no grandchildren and smooth the gay issue. She, no doubt, would be able to talk his father round in time.

★ ★ ★

For the first time in weeks Maria allowed herself to relax. Once released from questioning by the police, to which all the yacht's crew had been subjected, she had had two days before they found Cesare's body. In that time she had transferred to those accounts in her sole name all the money from his Cayman Island, Netherlands Antilles, Panama and Luxemburg tax-haven accounts, to all of which she was an authorised signatory. Initially she thought she might shut down the people-trafficking operation, but it was a stream of money for old rope, or in this case old boats, so she decided to continue it alone. She then cut a deal with Volpe. The two of them would have to leave alone all Romano Holdings' assets, but Volpe would assume control of some properties that had been registered through a Monaco shell company and appeared nowhere in the accounts.

Maria had already had her eye on a nightclub in Catania complete with bedrooms, which was struggling financially, having overspent on a refurbishment programme. She had heard about a casino in Palermo in similar straits. Both businesses would be ideal for laundering cash.

★ ★ ★

169

The Cardinal was as good as his word. The catacombs refurbishment was completed along with the visitors' centre, all paid for with Vatican money. Augusto enquired of it no further. The loss of the chest and letters was a great misfortune, although he suspected, as Verity had, that the world might not have seen them for a very long time had they contained controversial material. The last thing the Church needed just now was another scandal. The fresco which Giuseppe had so unfortunately, or fortuitously, fallen through was now revealed and restored. It was tentatively dated earlier than any of those frescos found in the catacombs in Rome. It depicted a bald, bandy-legged man with a mono-brow, his right hand raised in blessing. Something new for TripAdvisor.

CHAPTER 20

Epilogue

Catania and London

Enzo extracted the memory card and deleted everything on the camera's built-in chip. On a whim, he slid the card into his computer. Maybe he'd see pictures of its unfortunate owner, perhaps in a state of undress? Always good to know whom to avoid.

Picture after picture was more or less identical. He'd seen papyrus scrolls when he was taken on a school trip to Syracuse museum. Next door they had a workshop showing how they were made. He also recognised some Greek letters. All Sicilian children were instructed in their island's rich history. In some of the shots the writing looked different. It's all Greek to me, he thought. Every so often parts of hands holding the scroll edges were in shot. He's not done much manual work, thought Enzo, professionally pricing a little-finger signet ring. Getting bored, he skipped to the end. A couple were smiling, with Etna spewing in the background. They're probably not smiling now, he chuckled to himself. It was indeed a good camera.

Enzo was about to delete all the pictures, when some instinct stopped him. If someone had bothered to photograph all those scrolls, perhaps they had some value? Maybe he could sell them? Anonymously, obviously. He wondered if anyone had read them and where they were now. He might look into that. Extracting the card, he dug out a used envelope from the bin, wrote on it, 'Secret' and under that 'scrolls' and sealed it with scotch tape. Glancing round the room to find somewhere it wouldn't be disturbed, he pulled down from a high shelf his grandmother's Bible, placed the envelope inside and put it back.

★ ★ ★

One year later

Crispin rose to greet Verity as she entered an Italian restaurant just off Queensway in London. He noted that she'd lost weight since the last time he'd seen her and looked relaxed and happy. Both features he thought might be explained by the engagement ring she was wearing.

'You look great! Life going well?' he asked.

'Yes, very, I've just got engaged.'

'I noticed the ring. Many congratulations! Have you known him long?'

'Yes, but we lost touch until he came over from the States to work at Sotheby's.'

'Not a bandy-legged mono-brow I take it?'

Verity laughed and pulled out her phone to show Crispin some photos of Guidoriccio. 'Mind you, I think St Paul did me quite well considering. Not an adventure I'd wish to repeat, but it caused me to regain my faith. We're getting married in the Brompton Oratory next April. I'll send you an invitation. How about you?'

As she asked this Verity indicated a plain gold band on Crispin's fourth finger.

'Hilary and I got married in the summer. We had our reception in Corpus Christi College.'

'How did your parents take it?'

'Much better than I expected. You know that I was emboldened by that letter of Barnabas? When I got home, Hilary and I sat down and discussed how we might see our lives together long term. I then went back to my parents, still not sure how to tell them. After dinner one evening I showed them a photo of the two of us laughing together in a punt.

'My mother asked who my friend was. Taking a deep breath I said. "That's Hilary." There was a long silence, broken by a little sob coming from my mother. My father asked me why I hadn't told them before. I apologised but said that I wasn't sure how to, knowing their rather conservative views, and I didn't want them to be disappointed. I think they were a bit shocked that I had felt the need to keep it a secret from them. After a bit my father said, "Crispin I'd prefer you to be able to live your life openly. You know I don't really understand homosexuality, but I've seen too many of my clergy colleagues either living a lie with their 'good friend' or suffering loneliness and isolation by not being able to share their lives with someone. Being a vicar is isolating enough as it is." He took a deep breath and said, "I hope you'll be very happy together." Then he hugged me. The last time he did that was at Hector's funeral.

'My mother was still very upset until I explained that Hilary and I were considering adopting a couple of children. We are in the process of being vetted by the Coram Cambridgeshire Adoption Service. It was that which determined my timing for telling my parents, as the Agency wished to speak to them if possible. Ironically, my mother subsequently found that one of her bridge club members has a gay son, whose situation they had never mentioned, and that Victoria Radley, who runs the local Pony Club, had just married her long-term partner, Penny. She didn't feel so isolated after that.'

'I'm so pleased for you both,' said Verity. 'Going back to the scrolls, do you think that Gamaliel was ever convinced by Paul and actually became a Christian?'

'I doubt it. There is no evidence in the passing references to him in the Talmud, which is a collection of oral rabbinic traditions encompassing those of the first century, but written down after the destruction of the Temple in Jerusalem in AD 70. What have you done with your transcripts?'

'I've put them in a fire-proof box. I still can't believe I never downloaded the photos. I go hot and cold just thinking about them, though we would have had some very delicate explaining to do as to how we had made them.'

Crispin responded, 'I certainly wouldn't feel comfortable having to dodge the long arms of both the Italian legal system and the Vatican. I wonder if the pictures still exist?'

'Oh I imagine whoever got the camera would have formatted the memory card, so they could sell that on… Though you never know, maybe they will turn up one day?'

They lapsed into companionable silence as they ate.

Crispin asked, 'How's the job going?'

'Well, coming back from Syracuse was all a bit of a muddle, but Augusto assured the Foundation that the work was well in hand and would be completed with no further recourse to our funds, that they were extremely grateful for our help and would have a plaque mounted acknowledging the Poghosian's contribution. I think there'll be a little ceremony over there once all the work is completed.

'We've just been asked to contribute to the restoration of some icons in the Russian Orthodox Cathedral in Knightsbridge. I'm meeting up with them next week along with one of their benefactors. A man called Sergei Orlovsky.'

AUTHOR'S NOTES

The Hebrew word 'Messiah' and the Greek 'Christ' both mean 'the anointed one'. This would be the person anointed by God to bring salvation to the world; I have used the terms interchangeably, depending upon the context. The name 'Jesus' means saviour. It comes from the Hebrew Yeshua (יהוה), also having the variants Joshua or Jeshua.

When quoting Old Testament texts I have used the King James Authorised Version of the Bible, as in the first century AD the OT would have been an archaic language. However, when quoting St Paul's letters from the New Testament, I have used the New Revised Standard Version of the Bible, as the letters would have been written in contemporary Greek at the time.

Kairós, the Papal Commission for Sacred Archaeology, does manage the catacombs at the church of St John the Evangelist in Syracuse, Sicily, but all persons connected with it have been invented and bear no resemblance to real persons concerned with its administration. To my knowledge there have been no false walls discovered, although some of the tomb tunnels in the past were sealed up with walls decorated with frescos.

The Poghosian Foundation is an invention. The Armenian form of Paul is 'Poghos'.

In the ancient letters I have written God as G_d, to reflect the fact that the name of God was never written out in full in Jewish literature. What is known in Greek as the *tetragrammaton*, meaning 'four letters', is written in Hebrew as יהוה, commonly transliterated into Latin letters as YHWH which was turned into the name Yahweh or Jehovah.

Suggested further reading

The New Testament, preferably a modern English version, for example, the New Revised Standard Version or the New International Version.

Questions of Life, an Opportunity to Explore the Meaning of Life, Nicky Gumbel (Kingsway Publications, Eastbourne, UK, 1993). A text of the Alpha Course, www.alpha.org.uk, an introduction to Christianity.

Jesus: A Very Short Introduction, Richard Bauckham (Oxford University Press, UK, 2011).

The Gospels and Jesus, Graham N. Stanton (Oxford University Press, UK, 1989)

The Shroud: The 2000-Year-Old Mystery Solved Ian Wilson, (Bantam Press, 2010).

By the same author

Missing: Three Days in Jerusalem, S. Falaschi-Ray (Matador, 2013)

Harry Potter: A Christian Chronicle, S. Falaschi-Ray (Book Guild Publishing, 2011)

ACKNOWLEDGEMENTS

I should like especially to thank Professor Mirjam Foot, for her editorial advice and thoughtful comments, John Ingoldby for his editorial guidance and layout, Professor John Ray for his suggestion of an epilogue, Chris and Christina Rees CBE for help with character development and identifying plot-holes, Dr Dorothy Thompson for her advice on how one unrolls and translates ancient papyri and Professor Mary Beard for advice on grant-giving bodies for restoring ancient buildings. I would also like to thank the others who read drafts and offered much encouragement, Professor Mary Beard for advice on grant-giving bodies for restoring ancient buildings, as well as Susan Beer for proof reading.